Character sheet

write down the sentence from book

write definition
write your own sentence .
May 3rd
_____

character review

WHO IS
FELIX THE GREAT?

Also by Ronald Kidd

DUNKER

THAT'S WHAT FRIENDS ARE FOR

WHO IS FELIX *the* GREAT?

BY Ronald Kidd

LODESTAR BOOKS
E. P. DUTTON   NEW YORK

LIBRARY OF CONGRESS CATALOGING IN PUBLICATION DATA
Kidd, Ronald.
    Who is Felix the Great?

    "Lodestar books."
    Summary: When the fate of a once prominent person becomes the topic of an eleventh-grade English report, Tim chooses one of baseball's finest shortstops as his subject.
    [1. Baseball players—Fiction.   2. Mothers and sons—Fiction.   3. Single-parent family—Fiction]
    I. Title.
PZ7.K5315Wh   1982   [Fic]   82-7298
ISBN 0-525-66778-4   AACR2

Published in the United States by E. P. Dutton, Inc.,
2 Park Avenue, New York, N.Y. 10016
Published simultaneously in Canada by Clarke,
Irwin & Company Limited, Toronto and Vancouver
EDITOR: Virginia Buckley   DESIGNER: Trish Parcell

Printed in the U.S.A.   First Edition

10 9 8 7 6 5 4 3 2 1

to Paul and Ida Sue Kidd

WHO IS
FELIX THE GREAT?

Within the ballpark, time moves differently, marked by no clock except the events of the game. . . . Since baseball time is measured only in outs, all you have to do is succeed utterly; keep hitting, keep the rally alive, and you have defeated time. You remain forever young.

—ROGER ANGELL, *The Summer Game*

The old man lay on his back in the darkness. In one bony hand he cradled a transistor radio next to his ear. He muttered softly as he listened to the late-night telephone call-in show. He could barely hear what the callers were saying, because the battery was almost dead. He shook the radio and pressed it closer to his ear, but the sounds remained indistinct.

There were footsteps in the hall outside, and voices. The old man propped himself up on his elbows and shouted, "Hey, shut up out there!" He heard muffled laughter, and then the footsteps receded.

Bunch of fools, he thought. Bunch of loud, obnoxious fools.

He put the radio up to his ear again. It was completely silent. Cursing, he thrust it down onto the table next to him. For several minutes he lay rigid on the bed, fists clenched at his sides.

Then, staring into the darkness, the old man folded his hands across his chest and prepared to meet another long night alone.

Chapter 1

Tim heard the door slam. He braced himself for what he knew would follow.

"Julian!" bellowed Mr. Martinez from the front room.

It was a familiar ritual. First came the door slam, then the shout, then the sound of hurried footsteps clicking across the linoleum floor.

Mr. Martinez appeared in the doorway of the back room, where Tim was standing at a table, wrapping and labeling packages for shipping. Martinez was a small man with dark eyes that flashed like knife blades when he was angry.

"You've done it again!" the little man said. He slung an opened package onto the table in front of Tim. Inside was a broken toy. "That's the third one this week that was returned. You've got to start packing them better. I'm losing my shirt because of you!"

Tim never knew what to say when Mr. Martinez was on one of his tirades. He wanted to say the toys broke because they were cheap, not because of how they were packed. He wanted to say Martinez wasn't losing his shirt, his tailored slacks, his leather jacket, his imported loafers, his Cadillac, or anything else he had bought with the money that poured into the broken-down, two-room building every day. But he didn't, for the one thing that made Tim's boss angrier than finding broken toys was having people disagree with him.

"Well, what have you got to say for yourself?" demanded Martinez.

"I guess I'll try to be more careful."

"You *guess*? You'd better do a lot more than that, or you'll be out of a job." He turned to leave the room.

"Mr. Martinez?"

"What is it now?"

"I just wanted to remind you about this Saturday. My friends and I have tickets to a Dodger game, so I can't work that day."

"You just cost me a sale, and now you're asking for time off? You've got some nerve, kid."

"I told you about it before."

Martinez gestured as he left the room. "You're the expert, Julian. If you say you told me, who am I to disagree? Go to the game; what do I care?"

It was at times like this that Tim felt like quitting. He looked around the room. Small and cramped, it was lit

6

by a single bare light bulb. The rickety heater in the corner had never worked properly. The one window in the far wall had long ago been broken, and a sheet of plywood now covered it. The legs of the worktable were uneven, and Tim was constantly slipping pieces of cardboard under the short leg to keep the table from rocking.

But the worst thing about the job was his boss. Carlos Martinez never had anything good to say about anyone, especially Tim. From the day Tim had started work two years ago, Martinez had been on his back. At first Tim had taken every complaint seriously, thinking perhaps it *was* his fault. But then he began to realize Martinez was going to criticize him no matter what he did. So he tried to tune out his boss's shrill voice and just concentrate on the work. Sometimes he was able to succeed; other times, like today, he felt like flinging a handful of plastic toys into the man's face and stomping out the door.

Seeing that it was six o'clock, Tim picked up his schoolbooks from a chair and headed for the front door. On the way out, he passed through his boss's office. This was where Mr. Martinez wrote in the heavy ledgers each morning, recording every order that had come in the previous day's mail. The ledgers were stacked on one side of the desk. The other side was covered with pencil stubs, order books, and battered paper cups half filled with coffee. The more orders there were, the messier the desk became. This month, the desk was more cluttered than ever.

Tim switched off the light and locked the door behind him. He turned toward the curb, and there before him was proof that the job had not been all bad: his 1974 Dodge Dart. He had bought the car and fixed it up with money paid to him by Martinez.

As he often did before getting into the car, Tim stood there for a moment admiring it. The new white paint job glistened in the late-afternoon sun. The windows and chrome were spotless, and the hubcaps showed no sign of the dents he had hammered out.

He had bought the car four months before, shortly after his sixteenth birthday. At the time, some of the people at school had kidded him about buying a Dart. It was a tin can, they said. It had no power, no style. But Tim noticed that didn't stop them from asking for rides.

He climbed into the car and pulled away from the curb. Five minutes later he was home. As he walked up to the small white cottage, he felt the old familiar feelings coming back, layer by layer. There were feelings of warmth and security, because he loved the little house where he and his mother lived. It had been their refuge during the five years since his father had died. But beneath those feelings, there was always the sadness. For Tim, it had settled over the place five years ago and had never lifted.

"Hi, Mom," he called as he went through the door.

Bonnie Julian approached her son, stood on her tiptoes, and gave him a peck on the cheek. It would have been hard to tell at a glance that they were mother and son. He was a solid five foot ten; she barely came up to his chest. His hair, like his father's, was dark and curly, and his eyes were an intense brown. Her pale blue eyes and milk-white complexion were bordered by blonde curls that fell around her shoulders. But in spite of their obvious differences in size and coloring, mother and son shared certain subtle qualities: a particular way of lifting one eyebrow when puzzled, of pursing the lips when deep in thought, of blinking rapidly when upset. These were not so much physical similarities as signs of two people whose lives were closely intertwined.

"How was your day?" Tim asked.

"Fine. Just great!" she said over her shoulder as she went into the kitchen. "I represented our faculty at a district meeting on school vandalism."

Tim followed her into the other room. "Since when is vandalism such a cheerful subject? You sound like you just got back from a party."

"I did, in a way." She put four lamb chops in a skillet and switched on the burner. "I met a very nice man at the meeting. He's a teacher, too. We went out for a drink afterward."

"A drink? Isn't that rushing things a little?"

"Don't be silly."

"Mom, you're not used to this kind of thing. I'd go slow if I were you."

"Look, honey, I appreciate your concern," she replied, pulling two pots out of the cupboard, "but there's nothing to worry about. In fact, you should be glad—I'm dating again, and it feels great."

"Just be careful who you go out with, that's all. I'm not too impressed with this guy if he takes you out to some bar on your first date."

9

"I'll be the mother around here, okay?"

"I'm serious, Mom. This guy doesn't sound like your type."

"And just what is my type?" she asked, still working at the stove. After a moment, she turned and looked at him. "Oh, come on, Tim. Let's not go through that again."

"I thought you said Dad was the only man who could make you happy."

"Hey, I loved your father, and I don't need to prove it to anybody. But I don't intend to spend the rest of my life in mourning. I've got to start living again. Right now, that means dating Albert, so you'd better get used to it."

"Albert? His name is Albert?"

"Will you—" Suddenly she sniffed the air. She wheeled around and yanked a smoking skillet off the burner. Then she turned back to Tim and motioned toward the kitchen door. "Leave me alone. I can do without your help."

Chapter 2

Miss Molina wrote on the board, *Where Are They Now?* Then she faced her eleventh grade English class. "What ever happened to Neil Armstrong?"

"Who?" asked a girl in the front row.

"Neil Armstrong," someone said, "the first man on the moon."

"Does anyone know where he is today?" Miss Molina asked. No one answered. "What ever became of Nadia Comaneci?"

A boy raised his hand. "You mean that gymnastics girl? I think she got married."

"Do you remember Mark Spitz?" she asked. "Where is he today?"

"At the bank, counting his money," someone suggested. A few of the students laughed.

Janet Molina walked briskly back and forth in front of the class, her eyes dancing. Tim studied her from his seat in the back row. She was chunky, just a little over five feet tall, with dull brown hair and a small mouth. She wore her hair in a bun, so she looked older than her thirty years. She wasn't beautiful; she wasn't even pretty. But when she was teaching, she radiated energy. Tim was far from being the most active student in the class, but he counted himself among her loyal supporters.

"Did you ever have a favorite movie star who dropped out of sight?" Miss Molina asked. "A favorite singer or sports hero who disappeared? Well, now's your chance to find out what happened to that person."

She pointed to the board again. " 'Where Are They Now?' That's the name of our new unit. It will last until the end of the semester—about four more weeks. You'll be putting all your writing and thinking and research skills to work.

"Each one of you can pick a person you're interested in, someone you haven't heard anything about for a few years. Then you'll do some detective work to track that person down. You might want to look through old magazines or newspapers; you might check telephone directories; you might even want to do some interviews. Then, when you get a few solid leads, you can sit down and actually write the person a letter. At the end of the semester, you'll each prepare a report on your findings."

12

There were a few groans.

"Don't worry," she said, "you'll like it. It's like playing Sherlock Holmes. And don't get too upset about the report. If you do a good job on your research, the report should come easily.

"We've only got a few minutes before school's over. In the time we have left, I'd like all of you to start thinking about your subject. You can talk quietly among yourselves if you'd like."

Tim sat at his desk, watching his classmates huddle and exchange plans. He wanted to join in but didn't know what to say, so he slumped down in his seat and said nothing.

Five minutes later, when the bell rang, he hadn't thought of a subject for his report. He picked up his books and drifted toward the front of the room.

"Hi, Tim," Miss Molina said. "You seemed awfully thoughtful back there today."

He blushed. "Yeah, I was trying to come up with somebody really good for this project, but I couldn't think of anyone. Do you have any ideas?"

"It works better if it's your idea. But maybe I could help. What are some things you like doing?"

"Driving my car."

"What kind is it?" she asked.

"A Dodge Dart."

"I wonder who the designer was. I wonder who started the company."

"I don't know if I'd be interested in that," he mumbled.

13

"What else do you like?"

"Well, there's baseball."

"Do you have any favorite players? Is there anyone who's retired now . . . ?"

Something clicked in the back of Tim's mind. He looked off into the distance, then back at his teacher. "I'd better go. Thanks a lot, Miss Molina."

Tim hurried into his bedroom, dropped his books onto the bed, and pulled out the bottom drawer of his dresser. He searched through shoe polish and school yearbooks and combination locks and old magazines and iron-on decals. What he was looking for had to be right in front of him, if he could just put his hands on it.

And then he saw it. It was rolled up in a handkerchief. He unwrapped it carefully, and as he looked down at his prize, thought back to the first time he had ever seen it.

He had been seven years old. His father was teaching him how to play baseball.

"Great catch, Timmy! You're getting pretty good!" Tim's father caught the return throw. "Okay, here's a ground ball for you. See what you can do with it."

Tim turned sideways and stuck his glove out into the path of the baseball. The ball hit a bump and hopped over his outstretched mitt.

"That was a hard one!" Tim exclaimed, chasing after the ball.

14

"Here, let me show you something. Throw me a grounder."

Tim retrieved the ball and threw a high bouncer toward his father. Bob Julian half knelt in front of the ball, blocking its path with his big frame. The ball went right into his glove.

"See what I did, son? I got in front of the ball, instead of standing to the side. That way, if it took a bad hop it would hit my chest and I'd still have a chance to throw out the runner.

"You know how I learned that, Timmy? By watching the finest shortstop who ever lived."

"Who was that?"

"Felix the Great. Played for the Cubs in the thirties. He could get in front of any grounder hit within forty feet of him. When I was a kid, I used to see him play at Wrigley Field in Chicago. In fact . . ." Bob Julian glanced toward the house. "Come on, Timmy. I want to show you something."

Inside, Tim's father poked through his closet. He pulled an old shoebox down from the shelf and lifted out a round object wrapped in a handkerchief. He folded the handkerchief back to reveal a yellowed baseball. Written on the ball, in an awkward, childlike script, were the words

To Bob the Great
from Felix the Great.
Yours truly,
Felix Johnson

Bob Julian handed the ball to his son as though it were a piece of fine china. Tim cupped it in his palms.

"He was the greatest I ever saw," his father said. "Some people said he was mean. But he was nice to me the day I caught this foul ball. After the game I waited for an hour by the players' entrance. When he came out, I could tell he was in a hurry, but he saw me and smiled. I asked if he'd sign the ball for me. He said, 'Sure, kid, what's your name?' I told him, and he said, 'We'll call you Bob the Great. Just like me, Felix the Great.' He laughed and signed the ball. From then on, I was his biggest fan."

For Tim, there was something magical in that moment. He was too excited to know exactly what it was, but somehow it had to do with baseball, and somehow it was all bound up in that small stitched sphere that he cradled in his hands.

Now, nine years later, Tim gazed at the ball once again. Felix the Great. Felix Johnson. Who was he? Why had some people called him mean? How could a mean person have won Bob Julian's respect?

Tim walked over to the book shelf and pulled out his sports encyclopedia. He flipped to the *J*'s and found a picture of Felix Johnson.

It showed a young man with smooth skin and well-defined features. His Chicago Cubs cap was pushed back on his head, his well-muscled arms were crossed, and his dark eyes flashed a challenge to the world. His grin was more a smirk than a smile. The encyclopedia entry read:

Johnson, Felix Allen

Known as Felix the Great, Johnson was one of the most controversial players of his day. His fans described him as scrappy; his detractors called him everything from a punk to a street brawler. But there was no disagreement about his ability on the field: He was recognized as one of the finest defensive shortstops ever to play the game, and his hitting was nearly as good as his fielding. Johnson never backed down from any confrontation, whether with a beanballing pitcher or a sliding base runner. His pugnacious attitude got him into many fights, but it was also the driving force that transformed an athlete of only average skills into a player who could control the entire mood and tempo of a game.

Johnson played shortstop for the Chicago Cubs from 1927 to 1941. His lifetime batting average was .317, and during most of his career he led major league shortstops in fewest errors committed. He was on the National League All-Star team ten times, six of those in a row. After retiring, Johnson served for a brief time as a coach for the Boston Red Sox.

The player his father had cheered for at Wrigley Field would have been more than ten years older than the cocky young man who sneered up at Tim from the page. Tim wondered whether Felix the Great had mellowed during the later stages of his career. And he wondered what the man was like today—if he was still alive.

Tim intended to find out.

Chapter 3

Just two more rows, Tim thought.

Leaning forward, he pushed the lawn mower as fast as it would go. The blades whirred, throwing grass into the catcher. When he reached the other side of the yard, he turned the mower around and headed back toward the driveway. The last strip of tall grass disappeared under the wheels of his machine.

Quickly he pulled the catcher off the lawn mower and emptied it into a garbage can. He wheeled the mower into the garage with one hand, dragging the garbage can behind him with the other. The can skidded and scraped along the concrete behind him.

"What's all the racket?" his mother asked from the back door.

"Nothing," Tim replied. He pushed the mower and can into place against the garage wall.

Bonnie Julian smiled as she watched her son race through the kitchen and into his bedroom. "What's the hurry?" she called after him.

Tim grabbed his binoculars and the sports section of the morning newspaper. Halfway to the front door, he stopped and turned to his mother.

"I'm going to a Dodger game today, in case you've forgotten," he said. "I have to pick up Michael and Cal. See you later." He made a quick exit before she could reply.

He opened the door of his car and slid in, dumping his things into the back seat. The engine started with a roar, and he shot off down the street toward Michael's apartment.

A year ago, he thought, his mother would never have forgotten something as important as a Dodger game. She would have been as excited as he was. But now all that had changed. Now she was always off someplace, running around with people like this Albert.

He pulled up in front of Michael's place, his brakes squealing. Michael sat on the front steps, his head buried in a copy of *The Sporting News*.

Michael Morgan was a lanky, young man whose dark brown face often had the dazed expression of a sleepwalker. There were people at school who thought there was something wrong with him, but Tim knew better. It was just that Michael spent half his time in another world—a world of batting averages, pitching

19

records, and won-lost percentages. Michael was addicted to baseball. He was a Dodger junkie.

Tim jammed his palm onto the horn. Michael's head shot straight up, and his paper fell into a heap. Looking at his friend, Tim found his anger dissipated and he began to laugh.

Michael got into the car. "Very funny, man."

"Sorry, Michael. I guess my hand slipped." He pulled back out into the street and turned at the next corner, going toward Cal's house.

"Did you bring it?" Michael asked.

"Bring what?"

"The sports section."

"Oh, yeah, right." Tim motioned with his head. "It's in that pile of things on the back seat."

Michael quickly located it and began reading the front-page story on the Dodger game. His family subscribed to the evening newspaper, so he often borrowed the morning sports section from Tim. In Michael's opinion, there was no such thing as too much sports news.

As Tim turned onto Cal's block, he saw that this time there would be no need to honk. Cal stood at the curb, motioning for them to hurry up. He was short and stocky, with brown hair that he liked to slick back behind his ears. Today he was wearing powder-blue polyester pants and a yellow golf shirt.

Cal stepped out to meet the car and jumped into the back seat. "We're running late. Let's go."

"Do you have the tickets?" Tim asked.

Cal answered by pulling a small envelope out of his

shirt pocket and waving it in front of Tim's nose.

"All right, all right," Tim said, brushing the envelope away. He turned the car around in Cal's driveway and started back in the other direction, going north on Echo Park Avenue.

Cal leaned forward and looked over the front seat at Michael. "Hey, Sporting News, aren't you going to say hello?"

Michael grunted from behind the newspaper.

"You talk too much," Cal said. Then he laughed, because that's what people usually said about him.

Clarence Warren loved to talk, and what he most liked to talk about was California. Two years before, his parents had brought him west from New York. They had long since stopped referring to Los Angeles as a paradise, but somehow Clarence had never noticed. He just kept droning on and on, and his interminable sales pitch had earned him the nickname of Cal.

"Hey," he exclaimed suddenly, his elbows draped over the front seat, "who's going to win today?"

Tim guided the car north past Sunset Boulevard. "Save the cheerleading for later, huh, Cal?"

Cal hit Michael on the shoulder. "Hear that, Sporting News? Mr. Dodge Dart wants me to save the cheerleading for later. It's almost enough to make you think he isn't a loyal Dodger fan."

On his left, Tim passed some fast-food outlets and a schoolyard. On his right, small houses and courtyards were built into the side of the hill. At one corner was a blue-and-white sign in the shape of a baseball, with the word STADIUM and an arrow pointing to the right. He turned onto Scott Avenue and followed it up a hill, then down, then up another hill.

"Hey, Tim," said Cal, laughing too loudly, "they should make this a ride at Disneyland. What do you think, kid?"

Tim drove up one final grade and around a bend. And there before him was the most beautiful sight in the world: Dodger Stadium.

"What do you think, kid?" Cal repeated.

Tim gazed at the magnificent soaring curve of the grandstand and at the golden hills surrounding it.

"Cal, you talk too much," he said.

"I got it! I got it!" Cal screamed.

He and twenty other spectators converged on the aisle of the left-field pavilion stands where the batting-practice home run was headed. They crowded together, jockeying for position.

"Out of my way!" Cal yelled to a twelve-year-old, shoving him aside. Cal stretched to his left as far as he could and lunged for the ball. It fell several yards beyond his grasp, into the glove of a boy who couldn't have been more than ten years old.

Cal got up from the concrete steps and brushed himself off. "Just luck, that's all," he muttered. There was the crack of a bat, and once again Cal was off, pushing and shoving his way through the stands.

Tim leaned back in his seat, hands folded behind his head, and soaked in all the color and excitement of the ball park. He had heard that Dodger Stadium lacked the years of tradition possessed by some of baseball's older parks, such as Yankee Stadium in New York or Fenway Park in Boston. But for Tim, the park was filled with history. His father had started bringing him out to Dodger Stadium from the time he first knew what a baseball was. And after his father had died, Tim kept going to ball games, sometimes by himself, and sometimes with his mother or a friend. The games marked off the weeks and months and years of Tim's life, linking him with the days of his boyhood, and with his father.

Dodger Stadium was nestled in a ravine among rolling brown hills. The ball park was in the heart of Los Angeles, and yet, once inside the ravine, one would never know that just over the rise were factories and freeways. The grandstand was four tiers high, and three of the tiers extended from foul pole to foul pole. The vast majority of seats were in that area, and all of them had unobstructed views of the neatly kept field below.

But Tim didn't like to sit in the grandstand, behind the foul lines. He preferred the outfield bleachers, because these seats provided a player's view of the game. The action came directly toward you. It took place right in your lap—sometimes literally, if a long home run was hit. And it didn't hurt that these seats were the least expensive in the ball park.

Tim watched as the Dodgers trotted off the field after batting practice. Michael studied the players through Tim's binoculars. Behind them, Cal's voice rang out.

"I was robbed!" he cried, walking down the steps toward them. "That ball was coming right to me, and some guy jumped in my way."

Tim laughed. "I saw the play, Cal. That kid didn't jump in front of you. Besides, he couldn't have been more than four feet tall."

"But he was wearing a glove," Cal sputtered. "Do you see me doing that? No way. I use my bare hands. Otherwise it'd be like taking candy from a baby."

By the time the game began, over 50,000 people were jammed into the park. Those rooting for the Cubs had plenty to cheer about in the first inning, because the speedy Lambert reached base on a walk, went to second on a sacrifice bunt, and scored on a line-drive double that kicked up dust on the right-field foul line. Then, with two out, Torres sent a towering fly ball over the center-field fence, making the score 3–0. There were some shouts of approval as the Cubs finished their half-inning.

"Will you listen to those guys?" Cal said. "They live in the greatest city in the world, and they won't even support their own baseball team. I can't believe it."

When Torres trotted out to his position in left field, he was greeted by scattered applause. A nearby voice bellowed, "You're my man, Torres! Let's go get those Dodgers!"

Cal whirled around. Directly behind him, squeezed between the armrests of the seat, sat a huge black Buddha of a man. A beret was perched at an angle on his shiny head, and sunglasses with metal rims hid his eyes. The man nodded, flashing a smile that featured a gold tooth.

24

"How's it going?" he said.

Tim could see Cal draw back a little bit. "Okay, I guess," Cal said. "Why are you rooting for the Cubs?"

"I'm from Chicago. Who do you expect me to root for?"

"Well, I'm from New York," Cal said, getting his confidence back, "and you don't see me cheering for the Mets."

The man looked over at Tim and Michael. "What's his problem?" he asked.

"I don't have a problem," Cal said, "but obviously you do."

Michael rolled his eyes and turned back to his scorecard, leaving Tim to handle the situation.

"Don't let our friend bother you," Tim said. "He's running for president of the L.A. Chamber of Commerce."

"Looks like it," replied the man.

"Where in Chicago did you live?" Tim asked.

"North side. Right down the street from Wrigley Field, where the Cubs play."

"Hey, that's where my dad grew up. Did you like it there?"

"Sure did. There was nothing like that old neighborhood of mine. Hey, I bet you're a Cub fan, right?"

"Next to the Dodgers, they're my favorite team."

"Don't tell him that," said Cal.

"Turn around and watch the game," Tim replied.

Cal did just that, but he didn't like what he saw. The Cubs pulled farther and farther ahead, making the score 5–0, then 6–0. By the sixth inning they led 8–1.

"The Cubs are tough this year," the man remarked to Tim, the rims of his glasses glinting in the sun. "They got some muscle and some speed. And their pitching looks just fine."

Tim nodded. "I think they might win the division, don't you?"

"Right on."

Cal glared at both of them. Next to him, Michael kept his nose buried in the scorecard.

Two innings later, in the bottom of the eighth, the Cubs took the field leading 10-1. The man behind them struggled out from between the armrests of his seat and leaned forward. "No way the Dodgers can come back. I think I'll get going—try to beat the crowd out of here. Good talking to you."

"I enjoyed it, too," Tim said. All at once a thought struck him. "How long did you live in Chicago?"

"Thirty-five years—practically all my life. Why?"

"You seem to know a lot about the Cubs. Have you ever heard of Felix Johnson?"

"Felix the Great? Sure, he was one of the best. Too bad about what happened, though."

There was a roar from the crowd. Tim looked back at the field just in time to see a long fly ball headed right toward their section. The people around them jumped to their feet.

"I got it!" yelled Cal. He shoved his way past Tim and leaped for the ball. There was the slap of ball against hands. The next thing Tim knew, Cal was dancing in the aisle, holding his prize high over his head, grinning like a madman.

Michael looked over at Tim. "We're never going to hear the end of this."

Suddenly, Tim remembered the last puzzling words of the man sitting behind them. He turned around, a question forming on his lips.

The man was gone.

Chapter 4

Tim cleared his throat. "Excuse me."

The woman behind the desk looked up from her work. "Yes? May I help you?"

"Can you tell me where the baseball books are? I don't spend much time here."

"Are you looking for fiction or nonfiction?"

"Pardon me?"

"Do you want stories, or information about real players?"

"Real players."

"You'll find what you want against the far wall, in the 796s," she said. "And on the shelves next to me are the reference books. Look in the 796s there, too."

Tim thanked her and hurried across the room. He felt

uncomfortable in the school library. Shelf after tall shelf of books seemed to bear down on him, making him feel small and foolish. And he was certain that if his shoes creaked or his stomach rumbled, a hundred pairs of eyes would silently shout him down.

Usually, Tim spent his lunch hour in the cafeteria. But today he had a good reason to be in the library. The reason was Felix the Great.

He reached the shelf and scanned the numbers on the books: 700, 750, 790, 796. He read the titles to himself. Four of the books seemed to have possibilities, and these he took over to a table. One by one he looked through them, searching for any mention of Felix Johnson. There were a number of items about the former Cub, but none gave him any new information.

Tim replaced the four books and looked at some others on the reference shelf. Again, he found isolated paragraphs about the Cub star, but none helped very much. And there was nothing about any tragedy or even misfortune that might have prompted the man on Saturday to say that it was "too bad about what happened." That remark kept coming back to Tim. Had Felix Johnson gotten into some kind of trouble? Had he committed a crime? Had there been an accident or illness? Was Felix Johnson even still alive?

"Find anything?"

Tim saw the librarian nearby, seated at her desk. "Not really." He explained what he was looking for. She thought for a moment, flipped through some books on a low shelf behind her, and turned back to him.

29

"I'm not sure what to tell you," she said. "You've looked at everything we have, and I just checked the last sources I can think of. The only other thing ..." Her voice drifted off, and she touched her chin. "You might try the *Los Angeles Times*. They have a public information service where they track down facts for you." She picked up a scrap of paper, jotted down a telephone number, and handed it to Tim. "Sorry I couldn't be more helpful."

"That's okay. Thanks for trying." He took the slip of paper. "Maybe these people can help me."

Tim found a phone booth, dropped a coin into the slot, and punched out the number.

"*Times* information," said a voice at the other end.

"I'm trying to find out about Felix the Great," Tim blurted.

"Felix who?"

"Felix Johnson. He was a baseball player—"

"I'll connect you to our sports department." There was a click, and then another phone rang.

"Sports," a gruff voice answered.

"Have you ever heard of Felix Johnson?"

"Sure. Played shortstop for the Cubs in the thirties. Good ballplayer."

Tim felt his pulse quicken. "Do you happen to know what ever happened to him?"

"Seems to me he coached for a while."

"He was a coach for the Red Sox—I know that much. But what happened after that?"

"You got me, fella. Why don't you check the library?"

"I already did," Tim replied.

30

"You could always try writing directly to the Cubs," the man finally suggested.

"Do they answer letters?"

"I don't see why not."

Tim remembered something he had seen earlier. "Okay, mister, I'll try it. Thanks a lot."

He hung up and sprinted back toward the library. He stumbled into the room, out of breath, and as he did, the bell rang. Students all around him gathered up their books and started for the door. Tim pushed his way past them, straining to see the shelves on the opposite side of the room. And then he saw what he wanted: a row of telephone books.

He reached the shelf and pulled the Chicago book down. Flipping through it quickly, he found the listing: CHICAGO CUBS 1060 WEST ADDISON. He opened his notebook, tore out a sheet of paper, and copied the address and phone number.

By the time school was over, Tim had written four drafts of a letter to the Chicago Cubs. He had the drafts in his notebook when he got to work at two thirty-five that afternoon.

"It's about time!" said Mr. Martinez. "See if you can be here at two thirty tomorrow, just for the novelty of it.

"And by the way," he went on, getting up from his desk and walking into the back room, "do you have any explanation for this?" He pointed to the worktable.

"What do you mean?" Tim asked.

"This place is a mess! How can you get anything done when you're up to your knees in trash?"

Tim looked at the relatively neat worktable, then over Martinez's shoulder at the little man's own desk in the front room. Its top was covered with mountains of paper. "I'll clean it up this afternoon," Tim said.

"Make sure you do!" Martinez strode out of the room, picked up his leather jacket, and left by the front door.

Tim slung his notebook onto the worktable, then hit the table with his fist. Plastic toys bounced and rattled. He pushed his notebook to the side, and as he did, he noticed the sheet on which he had originally copied the Cubs' address. When he saw it this time, something different caught his eye—the phone number. Suddenly he knew exactly how to get back at his boss and find out about Felix the Great at the same time.

His watch showed ten minutes to three, which meant it would be ten minutes to five Chicago time. The Cubs' office might still be open. He took the sheet of paper, went to the telephone, and dialed the number.

"Chicago Cubs," said a woman's voice.

"I want to find out about a man who used to play for the Cubs."

"Just a moment. I'll connect you with player personnel." There was another click, and the ringing of a phone.

"Player personnel. Mrs. Carlton speaking."

"Maybe you can help me. I'm calling from L.A., but my dad grew up in Chicago, right near Wrigley Field. He told me about his favorite player, and I'm trying to find out if he's still around."

"What's the player's name?" the woman asked.

"Felix Johnson."

32

"Oh, yes, Felix Johnson is still very much alive, if that's what you mean."

"I've got some questions I want to ask him. Maybe you could answer some of them for me."

"Why don't you ask him yourself?"

"Is he there right now? In the office?"

The woman laughed. "No, he's not. He lives in Los Angeles."

Tim swallowed hard. "Felix the Great lives in Los Angeles?"

"That's right. He's been there for five or six years, I think."

"Can you give me his address?"

"Sorry," the woman answered, "but I'm not allowed to give out addresses. Why don't you look in the phone book? He lives on Alvarado Street."

"Yeah, I guess I could try that." He paused for a moment. "Can I ask you something? Is there anything wrong with him? Has he had some problems?"

Her voice sounded strange when she answered. "Oh, not really. I think maybe you should ask him. My goodness, we've been talking for over three minutes, and you're calling long distance. I don't want to run up your phone bill."

"It's no problem, really."

"Anyway, it's five o'clock here. I've got to get going."

"Hey, thanks. You've been very nice. So long."

Tim worked hard for the rest of the afternoon, hoping to make the time go fast and trying to overcome his nagging guilt feelings about using Martinez's telephone. By the end of the day, the worktable was completely

33

cleared, and on the floor next to it were two mailbags full of packages, ready to ship.

He sped home, parked hastily by the front curb, and raced into the house.

"Hi, Tim," his mother called from the kitchen. "Dinner in about five minutes."

He went to the kitchen door. "I'll be eating late tonight," he announced gruffly. "I've got something I need to do." Before she could answer, he grabbed the phone book and hurried into his room, shutting the door behind him.

He sat at his desk and opened the book. There, under the *J*'s, was what he was looking for: a Felix Johnson at 821 South Alvarado Street. After copying the address and phone number, he took out a fresh sheet of notebook paper.

> *Dear Mr. Johnson,*
>
> *My father's not alive anymore, but he grew up in Chicago in the 1930s, and you were his favorite player. You might remember him. He was the one who asked you for your autograph after a game one day, and you signed it on a baseball, "To Bob the Great, from Felix the Great." His name was Bob.*
>
> *I know you're probably very busy, but I would like it if you could find time to answer my letter. Could you please tell me what you have been doing since you left baseball? I'm very interested in this. What kind of work did you do? Where did you live? Did you ever think of becoming a manager? I think you would be good at it. What are you doing now?*

Tim wanted to ask if anything had gone wrong, but he was afraid that, if he did, Felix Johnson wouldn't answer his letter. He decided not to mention it and just hope there would be some clue in the return letter, if indeed there was a return letter.

> *Well, I guess that's about it. I don't want to take up any more of your time. Thank you for reading my letter.*
>
> *Sincerely,*
> *Tim Julian*

He wrote his address under his name and folded the letter. Then he took an envelope from the drawer and addressed it to Felix Johnson. He tucked the letter carefully inside, put a stamp on it, and hurried to the post office.

Chapter 5

It was the bottom of the ninth, and the fans were on their feet. Their rhythmic clapping and stomping rocked Wrigley Field.

Standing at third base, Felix Johnson looked up at the scoreboard. It showed Cubs 6, Cardinals 6. Felix, just ninety feet away from home plate, represented the winning run.

The pitcher looked in for the signal. Felix took a walking lead off third. He edged farther and farther off the base. The pitcher rocked into a full windup, and Felix took off for home plate.

By the time the ball was released, Felix was halfway there. The Cub batter, seeing Felix bearing down on him, backed hurriedly out of the box. The catcher grabbed the ball and positioned himself to block off the plate. Felix hurtled toward him and launched himself into a wide hook slide. The catcher leaned down on one knee and held the ball right in Felix's path. In a shower of dust, Felix kicked as hard as he could. The ball popped out of the catcher's glove, and Felix's left foot brushed across the corner of home plate. The Cubs had won the game, 7–6!

Felix's teammates poured out of the dugout and pulled him up out of the dirt. Surrounding him, they slapped him on the back and pumped his hand. The fans were on their feet yelling.

In the darkened room, the old man's eyes opened. He rolled onto his side and pulled the blanket back up over his shoulder. He closed his eyes again, but Wrigley Field was gone.

Muttering, he looked at the alarm clock. It was five in the morning. As usual, he had set it for seven o'clock, and, as usual, he had awakened long before the alarm went off. He knew he would get no more sleep now.

He put on pants, a frayed white shirt, scuffed shoes, and a tan sweater that buttoned in front. Running his hand through his wispy gray hair, the old man opened the door and stepped into the dimly lighted hallway. He shuffled down the hall toward the lobby.

"Morning, Mr. Johnson." Joe, the security guard, was seated behind the front desk, sipping coffee and reading the newspaper. "Up early again, huh?"

"Yeah," said the old man, not bothering to look at

Joe, "and I'm pretty sick of it." He pushed open the front door and walked down the sidewalk, then looked back over his shoulder. The sign next to the door said ALVARADO RETIREMENT HOME.

"Retirement home," he said to himself. "Why don't they just come right out and say it? It's an old folks' home. It's a place where people go to die."

He crossed the street and made his way slowly up the sidewalk toward the all-night market.

Later, Felix Johnson sat at one end of the sofa in the room they called the recreation room. He held the transistor radio to his ear, listening to a Saturday call-in-show.

When Felix had first gotten the radio, he had tried listening to it through a small plastic earplug. But people had mistaken the earplug for a hearing aid and had started raising their voices when they spoke to him. It had made him so angry he had thrown the earplug away. Since then, he had gotten into the habit of holding the radio up to his ear.

Sitting next to Felix on the sofa were Ina Rae Brown and Marvin Crosby. Brown was a tiny birdlike woman with a pointed nose and a voice like fingernails scratching across a blackboard. Crosby wore a permanent sneer and liked to clean his ear with the smallest finger of his right hand. The two of them, along with several others seated nearby, were watching the end of a cartoon show on television. As the closing credits flashed onto the screen, Felix clicked off the radio and approached the television set.

38

"What are you doing, Johnson?" asked Marvin Crosby.

"What does it look like I'm doing? I'm changing the station." Felix turned the channel selector and made his way back to the sofa.

"And what if we don't want to watch your program?" said Ina Rae Brown. Felix dismissed her question with a brush of his hand.

"What's on?" Crosby asked.

"What do you think?" Felix snapped. "What do I watch every Saturday morning at eleven from April to September? Baseball, that's what."

Ina Rae poked a sharp finger at his arm. "That's three hours long! You can't watch that!"

Before Felix could reply, a chubby pink-faced woman came into the room. Elizabeth Crawford, like the rest of them, was a resident of the retirement home. She helped in the office every day, her main job being to sort the mail. Recently she had been throwing friendly glances in Felix's direction.

"Mr. Johnson," she said, "I thought you might want this." Smiling warmly, she handed him a letter.

A look of surprise flickered across his face but was gone as quickly as it came. "Last time I checked, I had a mailbox. Put it in there next time." He snatched the letter from her and turned back to the television set. She didn't move. "Well, what are you waiting for? I'm trying to watch a baseball game." Her smile fading, Elizabeth Crawford left the room.

"Hey, Johnson," said Marvin Crosby, "since when do you get personal mail service?"

39

Ina Rae snorted. "She couldn't put it in his mailbox because the box was filled with cobwebs."

Without looking at the envelope, Felix set it down on the sofa next to his leg. He peered back up at the television screen and forced himself to watch four full innings of the game. In the top of the fifth, he reached down and picked up the letter again, trying to look nonchalant. He was surprised to see it addressed in the awkward handwriting of a young man.

His hands trembled as he tore off a narrow strip at one end of the envelope. He pulled out a sheet of notebook paper folded in thirds and opened it up. Felix read the letter, slipped it back into the envelope, and put it in the pocket of his shirt.

He turned to Marvin and gestured toward the television set. "The Red Sox are going to come back and win this game, Crosby. You just watch."

"Who says so?"

The old man's eyes flashed. "Felix the Great, that's who."

Chapter 6

"So the next thing I know, she says, 'Why don't you ask him yourself? He lives in Los Angeles.' " Tim was sitting on a low brick wall outside Wilson High School with Cal and Michael. "I couldn't believe it. I'd been trying to track the guy down, and all the time he lived right here."

"What did you say this guy's name is?" Cal asked.

"Felix Johnson. They called him Felix the Great. He played shortstop for the Cubs in the thirties."

"Oh, yeah? Hmmm."

"He was always hustling," Tim continued, "pushing for an extra base, diving to knock down ground balls. Sometimes he got into fights, but it was just because he tried so hard. He had a lifetime batting average of

.317, and he was even better at fielding than hitting. You don't hear much about him, but he was a great player."

Michael yawned, his eyes glazed behind the thick glasses. He turned his head slowly and stared off in the other direction.

"I decided to write a letter to this guy," Tim said. "I asked him a bunch of questions so when he writes back I can do a report for Miss Molina. But in a way I'm not interested in the report anymore. I just want to find out what happened to Felix Johnson. I wish he'd hurry up and answer my letter."

"Hey, there's one of those new Porsches," Cal exclaimed.

Michael blinked and squinted through his glasses. "All right!"

Cal looked back at Tim. "What do you think, kid? That car looks great, huh?"

"Cal, what have I been talking about for the last five minutes?"

"Felix something. Felix Jackson."

Tim looked at his other friend. Michael shrugged.

"See you later," Tim grunted, striding off toward his car.

"Hey, don't we get a ride?" Cal yelled after him.

Tim kept on walking.

When he got home, the first thing he checked was the mailbox. It was empty. He went into the living room and picked up the sports section of the newspaper.

A few minutes later Bonnie Julian came into the room, taking off her gardening gloves. "Weren't you supposed to work this afternoon?"

"No."

"Is there some problem with Mr. Martinez?"

"Yes, there's a problem with Mr. Martinez," Tim said from behind the paper, "but that doesn't have anything to do with why I'm not working today. My day off this week is Wednesday, that's all."

"Look, Tim, I don't mind your being in a bad mood, even if it has lasted two weeks. But I do mind your taking it out on me. Especially when I'm trying to be sympathetic."

"Yeah, okay," he replied, still reading the paper.

"I bought some steaks on the way home. Would you like to cook them on the grill?"

"I don't know. I have a lot of homework tonight."

"I bought a pie, too. It's banana cream—your favorite."

He sighed. "Okay. But I need to do some homework first. It'll take me a while to get to the steaks."

Two hours later, Tim stood next to the grill in the backyard, watching the smoke drift up through the trees. His mother leaned out the door. "How are they coming?"

"Almost done."

"I'll put the salad on the table. Come on in when you're ready." She went back into the kitchen, and Tim followed her a moment later, carrying two charbroiled steaks on a platter.

43

The meal began without a word, but soon Tim's mother broke the silence. "We haven't done this for a long time."

"Nope." As Tim poured dressing over the salad, he could feel her gaze. "You've been pretty busy," he said.

"We've both been pretty busy. Tim, I hate it when we're not speaking. Why don't you tell me what's bothering you?"

Tim didn't want to talk about Albert. But to his surprise he found that he did want to talk. "I guess I'm mad at Cal and Michael. Sometimes they don't listen to what I'm saying."

"I'll listen."

Tim started to tell her about Felix Johnson, but somehow it didn't seem right. "Oh, it was just some school assignment."

"How is school these days? You spend a lot of time on your homework."

"It's okay. I'm probably getting Bs and Cs in all my classes."

"How about in between classes? Have you made any more friends?"

"Some, I guess. But mostly I spend time with Cal and Michael. Anyway, with school and my job, I don't have much time to meet anybody else."

"Tim, you don't have to keep the job if you don't want to. I've told you, now that I'm teaching full-time, we could get along without your income. I'd rather see you having fun in the afternoons than working."

"I want us to have a cushion in case anything happens. It makes me feel better to have extra money coming in."

"Well, it's up to you. But that's your money. You can use it for college, or your car, or whatever."

"I won't need it for college. I'll be going to a junior college my first two years—tuition's practically free there, and I'll be living at home. Other than books, it'll hardly cost anything." Tim gulped down the last of his steak. "Where's the pie?"

She managed a smile and gestured toward the refrigerator. "Same old Tim. I'm glad."

He was just finishing his second piece when his mother said, "By the way, you got a letter."

"I did? The mailbox was empty."

"I picked up the mail when I came in. It's on my dresser."

Tim was out of his seat and on the way into his mother's room almost before she had finished. He picked up the mail and shuffled through it. And suddenly, there in his hand was what he had been waiting for.

It was an envelope on which Tim's address had been painstakingly printed. In the upper left-hand corner were the words *F. Johnson, 821 S. Alvarado St., Los Angeles, Calif.*

Tim opened it and lifted out the folded sheet of paper inside. He saw that the letter had been printed in much the same way as the address, by a hand that quivered slightly.

Dear Tim Julian,

I got your letter today. I get many letters. It is always good to know that people remember Felix the Great. I could hit, field, throw, run. I was colorful. I could get a crowd behind me, and not many of these new players can say that, with all their big salaries.

Baseball has changed. I think it's a shame. I watch games on television, and I can't believe how lousy some of these so-called "players" are. They don't give it an honest effort, the way I always did. They are too busy worrying about their bank accounts and their big cars.

Anyway, I could sit here and write down answers to all your questions. But it would be better for us to meet someplace and talk. How about this Sunday? I usually go to MacArthur Park on Sundays. I will be sitting on a bench near the band shell at two o'clock. I will be the one wearing the Cub cap and the tan sweater. If you don't come, I guess I can listen to the band concert. Even though most of the bands they get are terrible.

Felix the Great Johnson

"What's the letter?" his mother asked from the other room.

"Oh, nothing, Mom."

Tim let out a silent cheer, jumping and hopping around the room, throwing his hands into the air. Then he folded the letter up, put it into his shirt pocket, and walked back to the kitchen, trying to act as if the world were just the same as it had been five minutes before.

46

Chapter 7

MacArthur Park is at its best on Sundays. The things that seem run-down during the week—the buildings, the concession stands, the benches, the low stone walls—appear merely quaint when the bustling commuter crowds are gone and the park is given back to the very young and the very old.

A warm breeze blows, and the stagnant pond becomes a peaceful lake. Couples float lazily in rented boats, their voices drifting over the water. The rumpled regulars sit idle, as usual, but on Sunday they blend right in: The rest of the world has slowed down to match their pace.

On that particular Sunday, Felix Johnson walked down the path toward the west end of the park. His

deep-set brown eyes stared straight ahead, barely notic-
ing the groups of people on either side. He walked past a
couple lounging in the grass, between two young girls
jumping rope, through the infield of a softball game.

"Time out!" yelled the first baseman. "Hurry up, old
man! You're in the way!"

"I'll hurry up if I feel like it! I've never been chased off
a baseball field in my life!" On any other Sunday he
would have slowed down just to spite the young man,
but today he kept going.

As he started up a slope toward the band shell, he
heard a gravelly voice. "Hey, Felix, come on over. I got
the Dodgers on the radio." It was Sid, gray-haired and
frail. Felix often sat with him and argued baseball to
pass the time on Sunday afternoons.

Today he waved Sid off. "I can't—I'm in a hurry." He
pushed up the sleeve of his tan sweater and pointed to
his wristwatch. "I have an appointment. Soon."

"You got an appointment? In MacArthur Park?
Wearing a baseball cap?" Sid laughed, shoulders heav-
ing, and the laugh turned into a hoarse cough. Felix
walked on.

As he rounded the edge of the band shell, he saw a
group of about fifty uniformed musicians. Scattered
across the lawn in front of them was an audience of perhaps a hundred people—listening, talking, knitting,
yawning, or just leafing through the pages of the Sunday
newspaper. Nearby was a wooden bench, and that was
where Felix headed.

He sat down and began fidgeting and glancing at his

watch every few seconds. It was 1:30, then 1:40, then 1:50.

"Mr. Johnson?" asked a voice just behind his left shoulder. Felix started. He spun around to face a curly-haired young man. "I'm Tim Julian. I wrote you a letter, remember?"

"You didn't have to sneak up on me like that." Tim's nervous smile sagged. Felix gestured toward the path he had been facing. "I was expecting you from that direction. You shouldn't have come up behind me."

"I'm sorry. I didn't mean to scare you."

"Scare me? Young man, I've had pitchers throw at my head and base runners try to spike me more times than I care to think about. I'm not about to be scared by some teenage boy." Tim drew away, his face flushed. Felix motioned toward the bench. "You might as well have a seat."

Tim sat on the edge of the bench, hands folded stiffly in his lap.

"I suppose you want to hear all about me," Felix said. "Everyone does. I'm always getting letters pestering me with questions. 'What kind of glove did you use?' 'What was the best game you ever played?' 'Were you better in the field or at bat?' 'When did they start calling you Felix the Great?' Well, I've got better things to do than answer letters all the time."

"It was sure nice of you to answer mine so quickly."

"You caught me on a slow day."

"Do you remember my dad?" Tim asked.

"What do you mean?"

49

"You know—in the letter, I asked if you remembered signing my dad's baseball when he was a boy. You called him Bob the Great."

"Oh, yeah," the old man replied. "People were always asking for my autograph. That's because I was the best. Oh, there were others with more natural ability. But I *made* myself a great player. The fans appreciated that, and they let me know every time I walked out onto the field."

Tim rubbed his damp palms together. "Mr. Johnson, I wonder if I could ask you something. I know all about your career—"

"No, you don't. You had to see me to know how good I was."

"Well, let's just say I've read a lot about you. But I could never find out what happened after you stopped playing."

The old man glared at Tim. "They fixed it so I never had a chance."

"What do you mean?"

"I wanted to be a manager, and I told the Cub front office during my last season—that was '41. I knew I could be a great manager, because I'd learned about baseball the hard way—by teaching myself. I told them I'd be willing to start as a coach and work up to managing.

"The front office tried to discourage me right from the start. They said I was too controversial, said I didn't get along with people. That wasn't true, and they knew it. The fans loved me. Course, sometimes I did get into arguments with the other players. Everybody did sooner or later. But the front office had branded me a trouble-maker, and that was that." Felix turned and spit into the grass.

"At the end of my last season, I went around to see about other coaching jobs. I tried the National League teams first." He waved his finger in front of Tim's nose. "And you know what happened?"

"No, sir."

"Every team in the National League turned me down! Think about that for a minute. Here I was an All-Star, a man who knew baseball inside and out, and the teams weren't interested. It didn't make sense. When I pressed them, they all said the same thing—I was a trouble-maker. Well, it was obvious what had happened. The Cubs had blackballed me!"

"Maybe—"

"Maybe nothing! It was as plain as day. I wasn't going to let it stop me, though.

"I went to the American League teams next, figuring maybe the Cubs hadn't gotten to them. But I was wrong. One after the other, they told me I had a bad reputation. One of the last teams on my list was the Boston Red Sox. They turned me down, but a few days later one of their coaches retired. By that time spring training was near, so they wrote and said they'd take a chance on me. *Take a chance on me!* Well, I thought about turning them down on principle. But I didn't know if I'd get any other offers, so I decided to accept."

"You must have been pretty happy to finally get something."

"Happy! I was furious! I'd been insulted by nearly

51

every team in the big leagues, and now, when I did get a job, it was offered like some kind of charity." Felix yanked at the bill of his cap. "Oh, no, I wasn't happy, I can tell you that. But I did take the job."

"How did it go?" Tim asked. "I mean, when you actually started coaching."

"Terrible! The manager, the players, the other coaches—nobody would listen to me. They had their own way of doing things, and by God, no one was going to change it. The week before spring training, I told the manager how things should be run. I gave him some good ideas, too, ideas I knew would work. But he said he already had things planned. I asked him what the plans were, and he told me. I went through each point and explained why my ideas were better, but he was too stubborn to listen.

"Now I'm not the type of guy who likes to push himself on people, so I didn't press the issue. When spring training started, I just did my job. For instance, whenever the players did something wrong, I'd tell them how to do it the right way. They'd just look at me funny and walk away.

"It went on like that for the rest of spring training and the first part of the season. I was getting so mad I could hardly see straight. Everything I said was ignored, like I was crazy or something."

"What finally happened?"

"There was a weekend series in Detroit. We were battling them for last place, which gives you some idea how much the team needed my help. Well, anyway, I was hitting ground balls to the infielders before the first game started, like I always did. I hit one to Weatherspoon, the shortstop, and it went right under his glove. I shouted to him, 'You'll never be a big leaguer, Weatherspoon, and neither will the rest of these stiffs! You *belong* in last place.' He shouted back, 'At least last place is still in the majors. You belong in the bush leagues.' I told him to come closer and repeat what he said. He did, and I decked him."

"You mean you punched him?"

"That's right."

"On the baseball field, in front of the crowd and everything?"

"The man called me a bush leaguer right to my face. Besides, he and his buddies had been wising off to me from the beginning."

"Was he hurt?"

"Nah. Just a bloody nose was all. But from the way the manager acted, you'd have thought I'd committed murder. He ran up and started screaming about it being the last straw. He made me follow him into the clubhouse, and down there he screamed at me some more. Then his voice got quiet all of a sudden, and the next thing I knew he was telling me I was fired. Fired! Me, Felix the Great, let go like some third-rate utility infielder!"

Behind them, the music faded away. The crowd applauded and began drifting out of the area, past the bench where Tim and Felix sat.

"I guess you probably want to know what happened

after that," said the old man. "Well, I'll tell you—nothing. That was the end of my career in the big leagues. I never worked in baseball again."

Chapter 8

Dodger Stadium loomed in front of them, blue and white against the cloudless sky.

"You mean you've never been here?" Tim asked Felix as they walked across the parking lot.

"That's right," the old man answered.

"But you live so nearby. I would think you'd be coming here all the time, being a former player and all."

"Maybe I didn't feel like it."

"Okay, just curious."

It had been three weeks since Tim first talked to Felix Johnson. In that time, Tim had written his paper for Miss Molina, and the school year had ended. To Tim, summer vacation meant baseball, so he had lost no time inviting Felix to Dodger Stadium. They had met at Mac-

Arthur Park, and Tim had driven to the stadium.

He pointed to an entrance. "That's where we go."

"How do you know?" Felix asked. "You already have tickets?"

"Yeah, I bought some reserved seats for us a few days ago." Tim didn't say so, but it was the first time he'd bought tickets for any place but the outfield bleachers. He wanted to make it a special occasion, so he'd splurged on the more expensive seats.

He pulled the tickets from his pocket. "Don't those cost a lot?" asked Felix. "I'm not rich, you know."

"I'm paying. You don't have to worry about a thing."

A look of genuine surprise crossed the old man's face. But the look was gone as quickly as it came, replaced by the same dogged expression Felix usually wore. "Fine with me," he mumbled.

They went through the turnstile and headed for their seats. As they made their way down the aisle, Tim was amazed to see how close home plate looked. They found their places and sat down.

"Good view, huh?" Tim said. "Right between home and first base."

Felix didn't answer. He was watching the field, and his eyes were glistening. "I always liked batting practice." He pointed at the players clustered around the batting cage. "Look at them down there—talking, joking, telling stories, just like we used to do. There's something special about the time right before the game. You practice your hitting, sure, but there's more to it than that. It's almost like being a kid again. You play catch, you take a

56

few swings, you jog around on the grass. Oh, you know in the back of your mind that you're living out of a suitcase, that you'll go back to the hotel after the game and sit by yourself in your room. But for that hour or two before the game, you don't worry about any of that. You get money for playing ball, but this"—he gestured toward the field—"this is the real reason you do it. At least it was in my day."

Tim was thrilled by the unexpected outburst. Maybe this was the real Felix the Great.

Then Felix's expression hardened. "Baseball's changed. The players are rich mamma's boys. They're more interested in reading *The Wall Street Journal* than in playing ball. They don't hustle or care about the fans. All they care about is themselves."

The game was soon under way. The Dodgers were playing the Houston Astros. Felix was familiar with all the players and made comments about them as they stepped to the plate, saying how one player had a hitch in his swing, another was trying for a home run on every pitch, and still another might hit thirty points higher if he'd just learn how to bunt.

"Look at that McCormick," he stormed. "He calls himself a shortstop, but he can't move to his left for beans, and he needs practice turning the double play. In my day, they would have kept him in the minors until he learned those things. Now, they not only bring him up before he's ready, but they pay him a king's ransom on top of it. That bum makes five times what I used to make."

57

During the seventh-inning stretch, Felix looked around at the stadium itself. "This place looks like a factory, not a ball park. It's too clean; it's too cold. Look at these seats—plastic. Seats in a ball park should be made out of wood. Have you ever been to Wrigley Field in Chicago?"

"No, but my dad went there when he was a kid. That's where he saw you play."

"Wrigley Field has ivy growing on the outfield walls," Felix said. "Sometimes the ball hits the wall and just disappears among all those leaves and vines. If the outfielder can't get it, it's a ground-rule double. Probably two or three of my doubles are still in there.

"Fenway Park in Boston's another one. It's got that short left field with the high fence. All those old parks have their quirks, and that's what made them interesting. This place has nothing. It looks nice, sure, but it doesn't have any personality."

In the eighth inning, it was the uniforms that drew a blast from Felix. "Look at those Houston outfits. They look like something you'd find in a fashion store. They don't even have a fly. No zipper! You pull them on like panty hose!"

The game was a close affair. The Dodgers went into the bottom of the ninth, trailing 3–2. Their first man up doubled, but the next two struck out and popped out. Then the Dodger second baseman, light-hitting Jorge Antillo, stepped to the plate.

"They should pinch-hit for him!" exclaimed Tim. "He's struck out twice already today."

Felix shook his head. "No, the manager's doing the right thing. This kid's got potential, and he's never going to reach it if they don't give him a chance in tough spots."

"Come on, Jorge!" Tim yelled. Out of the corner of his eye, he saw Felix leaning forward a bit, his eyes glued to the field.

The first pitch was a strike. The second was a ball, low and outside. Antillo backed out of the box and got a handful of dirt. The fans, some of them on their feet, were shrieking for a hit.

The runner led off second. The pitcher rocked into his motion and delivered. There was a loud crack as Antillo's bat hit the ball, and suddenly the left fielder was sprinting for the wall. When he reached the warning track, he turned and looked over his shoulder. The ball sailed high over his head and into the stands. It was a home run! The Dodgers had won, 4–3!

Tim jumped in the air, holding his fist high, cheering along with the rest of the big crowd. Antillo touched home plate and was greeted by his teammates. The happy group trotted into the dugout, but the cheering did not stop. The fans wanted Antillo to come back out.

Felix, who had remained seated up until now, slowly got to his feet and started clapping in hard, deliberate strokes. He craned his neck to see the dugout, and his face was flushed. Finally, Jorge Antillo came up the steps of the dugout, took off his cap, and waved it to the crowd. The people roared their approval.

The cheering died down, and the crowd began to leave the stadium. Only Felix stayed rooted to his spot, smiling, clapping, a faraway look in his eyes.

Chapter 9

Tim drove slowly down the right-hand lane of Alvarado Street, straining to see the numbers on the buildings. MacArthur Park had been the 600 block, and now he was in the 700s.

The envelope in which Felix Johnson's letter had come was on the seat beside him. Tim read the return address: 821 S. Alvarado St. It was Thursday afternoon, a week after the ball game, and Tim had decided to drop in on Felix and surprise him.

He drove past another street and onto the 800 block. Judging from the return address on his letter, Felix's house should be just a few doors down.

Tim parked at the curb in front of 811. It was a small but well-kept apartment building. Felix's place, he decided, must be very much like this one. Probably the old man didn't own a house at all; it was more likely he rented a small flat or apartment. Tim locked the car door and hurried down the sidewalk. Number 813 was a locksmith's shop; 815 was a beauty parlor; the space where 817 and 819 should have been was nothing but an empty lot.

Then Tim saw the side of a building that bordered on the lot. The top layer of paint was pink, but that had chipped away to reveal a dingy green color beneath. As he came up even with the building, he saw a dirty glass door on the front with the number 821 stenciled on it. Next to the door was a sign that said ALVARADO RE-TIREMENT HOME.

Thinking he had misread the envelope, Tim glanced down at it again. But 821 was indeed the correct address.

Tim entered and approached the front desk, where a plump woman sat reading a copy of *Reader's Digest.*

"Pardon me," said Tim, "I think there must be a mistake. Felix Johnson doesn't live here, does he?"

The woman smiled. "Felix Johnson? He most certainly does. I'll get him for you." Before Tim could stop her she disappeared into the next room.

While Tim waited, he crumpled the envelope and jammed it into his pants pocket. His hands darted from his belt to his chest to his thighs like a pair of frightened birds.

The woman came back into the room. "I just spoke to him over the intercom and told him he had a visitor. He said fine, that he was expecting someone, and to send him on through. But I know who he's expecting, and it's not you. So let's surprise him, okay?"

Tim started to object, but the woman stopped him. "It's all right," she said. "I'm a good friend of his. He won't mind." She beckoned to Tim with one finger, like a child playing a game. Not knowing what else to do, he followed.

They went down a darkened hall and through a cramped room that had a TV set, several rickety card tables, and a sofa. Old people—incredibly old people, Tim thought—were huddled singly and in groups of two and three. No one was talking. The only noises were the tinny sounds coming from the TV.

The woman led Tim into another dimly lit hallway. Their footsteps echoed on the linoleum floor. Smiling mischievously, she tapped on one of the doors. "Mr. Johnson, your visitor is here."

"I'm coming, I'm coming," said a gruff voice from inside the room. A moment later the door opened, and there before them, wearing wrinkled pants and an undershirt, stood Felix Johnson.

When he saw Tim, his scowl was replaced by a look of embarrassment. "What are you doing here?"

"I thought I might come by and surprise you," Tim said. This was not at all the way he had imagined it.

"But how—" Felix looked at the smiling woman. Some of his fire seemed to come back. "Wipe that grin off your face! And leave us alone." She backed up a few steps, then hurried off down the hallway.

Tim stood frozen in place, stunned by the angry outburst. "I didn't mean anything. I just wanted to surprise you."

Felix scratched his bare shoulder and looked down at his nightshirt. "I'll be right back," he blurted. He was back in a moment, buttoning a faded blue flannel shirt.

"When I answered the door," he said, "I thought it would only be my cousin. He comes by to see me sometimes. I don't want you to think I'm in the habit of wearing an undershirt when my fans visit. You know, you should have called before you came over. I can't have people barging in all the time. I'd never get anything done."

"Maybe I should go."

"You're already here. You might as well stay for a few minutes." Felix held open the door.

Tim's first impression was that the room looked like a prison cell. There were no windows, and the only furniture was a bed, a chair, a dresser, and a nightstand with a clock and lamp on it. Other than the telephone and a small transistor radio, there was nothing in the room that could even remotely be called a convenience.

But there was one human touch. On the walls were dozens of news clippings and pictures of Felix with the famous players of his day: Ruth, Gehrig, Hornsby, Cochrane.

"These are great," Tim said.

"They're nothing. Sportswriters don't know what they're talking about anyway. I've punched more than one in my day; should have punched more. When the Red Sox fired me from coaching, the papers made a big deal about how I'd gone off the deep end. Every writer in the country made me sound like a wild-eyed maniac. I went to a few myself and tried to straighten them out, but no one would listen. The owners had gotten to them first."

Felix sat on the bed, and Tim settled in the chair. "You told me what happened when you tried coaching. What about after that?"

"Well, the war was just starting, so I went down to enlist in the army. And *they* didn't even want me. Said I had a bad knee. Can you imagine that? They signed up every stiff who'd sat at a desk, but they didn't want Felix the Great."

"What did you do?"

"What *could* I do? All I knew was baseball, and baseball wasn't interested. So I looked in the papers for work. And there was plenty of it, especially in Detroit. They'd converted the big car plants over to tank production for the war. I figured if I couldn't help out in Europe or the Pacific, I'd at least do my part here. To tell you the truth, I needed the money, too. I never was very good at saving.

"I started to work at the GM plant, screwing in bolts on tanks. Real exciting work. Hard to take after having people cheer every move I'd made for fifteen years. There I was, stuck inside a building that smelled like motor oil, doing a job no one cared about. No, actually there was one person who cared—the foreman. He cared too much. That was the whole problem.

"One day he came up to me and said, 'Hey, Johnson,

we need you to work faster.' So I asked him, 'Who do you think you are, anyway?' He said he was the foreman and he was just doing his job. I told him that was good, because that's exactly what I was doing, and I could do my job a lot better without some ape looking over my shoulder. He didn't like that a bit. 'Who are you calling an ape?' he says. I poked him in the chest with my finger. He pushed my hand away, so I had to deck him."

"You did?"

"He gave me no choice. Besides, he had his eye on me from the beginning. He was upset because Felix the Great got more attention than he did. No one ever asked for *his* autograph."

"What happened after you hit him?"

"Oh, he went crying to one of the big bosses, and they fired me. I was glad to get out." Felix rubbed his hand across the stubble on his chin. "But it was the same everywhere I went. People couldn't handle the fact that I was famous. They wanted to knock me off my pedestal, so I had to get them first. Then I'd always get the blame.

"It went on like that. Sometimes I'd keep a job as long as six or eight months, but then, sooner or later, it would happen again. You wondered what I did after I left baseball? Now you know. I had thirty years' worth of two-bit jobs."

"How did you end up in California?"

"I have a cousin here, not that it matters much. California just seemed like a nice place to retire. I came out here seven years ago, when I was sixty-five."

His voice trailed off, and Tim could tell that his mind

66

was not on their conversation. "You know what I was just thinking about? The roar of that crowd at the ball game the other day. I'd almost forgotten how it sounded."

Felix leaned over to the nightstand, fished a scrap of paper out of the drawer, and handed it to Tim. It was a small newspaper article that had been neatly cut from the corner of a page.

OLD TIMERS' GAME

The Chicago Cubs announced today that their annual Old Timers' Game will be held at noon at Wrigley Field on July 4. The Cubs have a doubleheader with Pittsburgh after the Old Timers' Game.

Tim looked up from the article and saw that Felix was smiling. "I saw that in the paper two months ago," the old man said. "I hadn't thought about it until this past week. Then when I looked at it again, an idea came to me: The front office was never on my side, but the fans always loved me. I'll take my case to them. I'll step onto that field, and they'll let out a roar just like they used to. Then it won't matter what the front office thinks of me. It'll just be me and my fans." Felix's face glowed in the dim light. He gazed past Tim, past the faded walls, to a vision of Wrigley Field bathed in sunshine and crowded with cheering spectators.

"Did the Cubs invite you to the game?" Tim asked.

"No, they didn't," he snapped. "They never do. They hold an Old Timers' Game every year, and I've never once been invited. But this year I'll go anyway. And we'll let the fans decide whether or not I'm a star."

"July 4 is less than two weeks away," Tim ventured. "How are you going to get there?"

"Why, you'll drive me, of course," he answered.

Chapter 10

Tim stood at the worktable, packing plastic toys into cardboard boxes. He had been doing it for nearly thirty minutes, but his mind wasn't on his work. All he could think about was Felix Johnson.

It was Monday afternoon, less than a week since his visit to the Alvarado Retirement Home. Tim had spent much of his time since that day pondering Felix's astonishing suggestion about driving to Chicago.

He had always dreamed of going there. Over the years, his father's stories had almost convinced Tim that it was his own home town. The old brick buildings, the downtown Loop, the chilly winds off Lake Michigan, the elevated trains, Grant Park, the first snowfall of the winter that would quickly turn to slush, summer heat that was thick with moisture, the ancient stone Water

Tower, and of course Wrigley Field—all those things, through his father's vivid descriptions, had become landmarks of Tim's own childhood. And now Felix the Great wanted Tim to drive him there.

"I can't just drive off to Chicago," Tim had told him on Thursday. "For one thing, I have a job."

"Jobs are a dime a dozen—I should know. You'll get another one when we come back."

"I've had that job for two years, and I don't want to lose it."

"Then take a vacation! Doesn't your boss believe in vacations?"

Tim shook his head. "He only believes in money."

"I don't get it. I'm offering you the opportunity of a lifetime, and all you can think about is your job."

"That's not the only problem. There's my mom. I have to be at home to help her out, because my dad's not around anymore."

"Just because your old man ran off—"

"He didn't run off. I told you in my letter—don't you remember?"

"Yes, of course I do. But we've got to start making plans. The fourth of July is a week from Sunday."

"I'm sorry, Mr. Johnson. I just can't go."

"You'll change your mind." He gave Tim his phone number and told him to call during the weekend.

Now it was Monday, and Tim still had not called. He wondered what he'd say when he finally got around to telephoning Felix Johnson.

His thoughts were interrupted by the sounds of the

70

front door opening and then slamming. The familiar brisk footsteps clicked across the linoleum floor. Mr. Martinez burst into the back room and glared at Tim.

"What's wrong?" Tim asked.

Martinez handed him the latest phone bill. A long-distance call was circled in red.

Tim's stomach tightened. He had meant to tell his boss about the call but hadn't gotten around to it. "I'll pay for it. Sorry I didn't mention it." He reached into his wallet and pulled out three dollars.

Martinez snatched the money and the phone bill. "That's all you're going to say? What about the merchandise that's been disappearing recently?"

"You think I stole some toys? Are you nuts?"

"I never did trust you."

"You actually think I've been stealing your crummy merchandise? What do you think I'd do, sell it on street corners? Hey, listen, go pack your own toys!" Before Martinez could answer, Tim brushed past him and out the door.

When he got home, he found his mother putting clothes into a suitcase. "Where are you going?" he asked.

"Santa Barbara. I'll be leaving tomorrow afternoon and getting back Thursday."

"Who are you going with?"

"Albert."

"You're going to Santa Barbara with Albert?" It wasn't so much a question as an accusation.

71

"Tim, you've got to accept the fact that you're not the only person in my life."

"Oh, I see."

"Don't you think you're just a little bit jealous?"

"That's ridiculous."

"I love you Tim. And I love Albert, too."

"Well, I wonder what Dad would say if he heard this."

She leaned forward and held his face tightly between her two hands. "Your father is dead! I've got to get on with my life!"

"Then don't let me stop you." Tim went into his room and slammed the door.

An hour later, he got up from his bed and walked to the desk. Holding a wrinkled scrap of paper in his hand, he lifted the telephone receiver and dialed a number.

"Hello," said a gravelly voice at the other end.

"Mr. Johnson, this is Tim."

"Well, it's about time. When do we leave?"

Tim took a deep breath. "How does Wednesday morning sound?"

Chapter 11

I t was that time of day when the sun had not
yet come up, but things had started to glow.
Rooftops, hillsides, distant buildings and streets shim-
mered in the early-morning light. The sky had turned
from black to gray, and to the east, straight ahead, one
long, thin cloud was draped along the horizon like a pink
ribbon.

Tim flexed his fingers on the steering wheel and
glanced over next to him. Felix had propped himself
against the car door and fallen asleep. From his open
mouth came low, rasping noises in steady rhythm.

Just an hour ago, when Tim had picked him up, it had
all seemed like a great adventure. Felix had met him at
the curb, and they had put the old man's shabby suit-

case and shoulder bag in the trunk. "Let's get going," Felix had barked. "It's nearly five o'clock." They had sped off down the dark, empty street, headed east toward Chicago and the Old Timers' Game.

Now Felix was asleep, and the stillness had closed in around Tim. Felix's boasts and claims and descriptions of Wrigley Field had faded away, leaving just the steady hum of the engine and the old man's snoring.

It wasn't too late to go back. They weren't more than fifty miles east of Los Angeles. Tim could pull off the freeway at the next exit, turn left, and get back on going the other direction. By the time Felix woke up, they would be back at the Alvarado Retirement Home. And ten minutes later, Tim would be back at his own house.

He could even tear up the note he'd written this morning. It said:

> *Dear Mom,*
>
> *I'll be gone for a week or two. I'm taking a trip. There's no reason for me to stay around here. You'll be with Albert. And I don't care about Martinez and his job. I won't say where I'm going, but you don't have to worry. I'll be okay.*
>
> *Tim*

His mother had wanted to talk with him Tuesday afternoon before she left.

"Tim," she had called through the door to his room, "are you busy?"

74

"Yeah."

"Don't you think we'd both feel a lot better if we discussed things?"

"Maybe later," he replied.

She came back several times, and each time he put her off she sounded a little more worried. Maybe she had started to feel bad. Well, that was just the way it had to be.

Finally, Tim heard a car drive up front. "That's Albert," his mother called from the living room. Tim opened the bedroom door. "I really wanted to talk with you," she said. He crossed his arms, and she gave him a peck on the cheek. "I'll see you late Thursday afternoon. Maybe you and I can do something special Friday or Saturday night, okay?"

"Sure."

Albert came to the door and helped her with the suitcase. As she followed him down the walk, she glanced back at the house, then got in the car and slid across the front seat next to Albert. A moment later she was gone.

Well, Tim thought as he drove down the San Bernardino Freeway, now I'm gone, too.

He was on his way to Chicago—not just Felix's Chicago, but Bob Julian's Chicago. Tim had dreamed about it long enough. Now he would see what it was really like.

Felix woke up with a snort and a sputter. He slid up to a sitting position, stretched, and began to cough. When he finally stopped, he was panting with exertion.

"You okay?" Tim asked.

"Where are we?" Still gasping for breath, the old man squinted out the window, looking for landmarks.

"I figure we're almost to Barstow. Maybe we should stop there for breakfast."

Barstow, California, was a quiet little community in the Mojave Desert. Its weatherworn stores and houses squatted in the sun. Everything—buildings, trees, cars, sidewalks—seemed to be covered by a layer of brown dust.

On the edge of town Tim spotted a café. He pulled into a gravel parking lot occupied by several big semis.

The entrance to the little café was a screen door with a rusted Coca-Cola sign on it. Tim pushed his way through, and Felix followed close behind. Inside, two men sat in a booth, talking quietly and sipping coffee. At the counter was a third man. As he ate, he chatted with a middle-aged waitress who leaned against the counter, smoking a cigarette.

Tim and Felix sat down in another booth, and the waitress approached. "Coffee?" she asked.

"Lady, we just sat down," said Felix. "If you don't mind, we'd like a minute to read the menu."

"Hey, don't get excited."

"Just water for me," said Tim.

The waitress came back in a few minutes. "Ready yet? I wouldn't want to rush you."

Felix glared at her. "I'll take toast and two eggs, over easy. And try not to burn the toast."

"Pancakes and orange juice," Tim said.

She jotted what they wanted, then called the orders

through a window into the kitchen. When she returned to her conversation with the man at the counter, the two of them kept glancing over at the booth where Tim and Felix sat. Tim was glad he couldn't hear what they were saying.

"There's nothing worse than waitresses that talk back," Felix grumbled.

"She didn't mean anything."

"Well, it's a fine thing when a customer can't even place a simple order without being sassed."

"How far do you think we can drive today?" Tim asked.

"Huh? Oh, I guess Flagstaff or so. At that rate, we'll make Chicago by late Saturday. I figure it's a four-day trip."

"Where should we stay tonight?"

"The cheapest motel we can find. Fancy places are for front-office types. You and me don't go in for that stuff."

The waitress came over again, carrying two plates of food and a glass of orange juice.

"Where's my coffee?" Felix said.

"You didn't order any."

"You must be deaf, lady. I've had coffee for breakfast every day of my life. I'm not going to change now just because of you."

The waitress went to the counter, filled a mug with coffee, and brought it back. She slammed it down onto the table, causing the hot, black liquid to slosh over the edge and form a puddle around the base of the mug. She added up the bill, then went back to her conversation at the counter, gesturing energetically and nodding repeatedly toward Felix.

Tim was growing more uncomfortable by the minute, but none of it seemed to bother the old man. Felix gulped down the eggs and used the toast to sop up anything he had missed. In between bites he sipped coffee, making loud slurping noises. Tim ate quickly, figuring the faster he ate, the sooner they could leave.

When Felix had finished, he snapped his fingers at the waitress. She didn't move. He snapped them again. Finally she walked with deliberate slowness toward the table.

"I'm not a dog," she said.

"At least dogs come when they're called," Felix replied. "Bring me some more coffee."

The man sitting at the counter said, "Hey, watch your tongue."

Felix half rose from his seat in the booth. "Oh, yeah?"

"Maybe we should get going," Tim said.

"I think that's a good idea, sonny," said the man at the counter.

"Well, I don't!" Felix exclaimed, trying to scoot out from the booth. Tim put his hand on Felix's shoulder. The old man opened his mouth as if to say something, then closed it and headed toward the door. Tim paid the check and followed him out.

"Why in blazes did you stop me?" Felix demanded when they got into the car.

"Somebody might have gotten hurt."

"You're damn right. I would have beat his brains out."

He stared ahead, picking his teeth with his finger. "You've got to watch people, boy. You've got to watch them all the time."

They crossed the California-Arizona border shortly after lunch. On each side of the highway, the dry land stretched away toward mountains that were the color of baked clay. The only sights breaking up the monotony were boulders, Joshua trees, and an occasional rickety shack.

"You know, I almost didn't come on this trip," Tim said after driving awhile in silence.

Felix nodded absently.

"It's funny how quickly things can change. What did it was my mom. She went to Santa Barbara for a few days with a guy named Albert. She was real happy about the trip. Well, she won't be when she gets home and finds out I'm gone. My boss won't be too pleased either. I hope he's in that dingy room right now, packing toys and getting his clothes dirty.

"My mom's always telling me to stop worrying about my job and have some fun, so that's what I'm doing. When she finds out I'm gone, she'll have nobody to blame but herself. And Albert."

"I was married for a little while in my twenties," Felix said. "Didn't last long, though, because I was always on the road with the team. Course, even when I was home, we never got along too well. So we split up after six months. Next time I saw her, she was at a ball game with some guy who had slicked-back hair."

"Probably like Albert."

"She was hanging all over him. Made me sick."

"Santa Barbara. I can't believe it."

"What about Santa Barbara?" asked Felix.

"You know, Mom and Albert."

"Who's Albert?"

Tim pushed the accelerator to the floor, and the car lunged ahead through the barren terrain.

Chapter 12

Late that afternoon they left the desert and started climbing into the mountains. Cactus plants gave way to evergreens, and at last the air began to cool off. At seven thirty they entered the city limits of Flagstaff, Arizona. Its streets were well kept, and the rough wooden exteriors of the buildings gave the town a hardy Western look.

They drove slowly down the main street, searching for motels. Each one Tim picked out was promptly rejected by Felix as too fancy. Finally the old man found one he liked. It was a battered pink building with a sign in front that said CARLTON MOTEL. They walked up three rickety steps into the office.

81

"What do you want?" asked the woman at the front desk.

"We were looking for a room," Tim said.

"You from out of town?"

"Is this a motel or the police station?" Felix said.

"Okay, mister, I'm just doing my job." She reached into a drawer and laid a card in front of them. "Fill this out. That'll be ten dollars for the room—paid in advance."

A few minutes later, Tim and Felix entered an oversized closet containing two single beds and a rusted sink. Through a door to the left, they could see a toilet and old-fashioned bathtub.

"Let's get something to eat," Felix said. "We'll be spending enough time in this place later on tonight."

They went next door to a small diner and had sandwiches at the counter, then got into the car and drove through downtown Flagstaff. There was a neon sign with missing letters that said WEST RN POOL H LL.

"Pull over," Felix ordered. "I feel like shooting some pool."

As they walked in, they were greeted by the smell of beer and chalk. The whir of an air conditioner blended with low voices and laughter.

Tim picked a pool table away from the bar, because he didn't want anyone to notice he wasn't eighteen. Felix put a quarter in the slot. The balls rolled down, and he positioned them at one end of the table. They picked out cue sticks.

Felix chalked the end of his stick, looking around the

82

darkened room as he did it. "I'll break," he said. He gritted his teeth and punched the cue ball solidly toward the pack. There was an explosion, and the balls flew in all directions, bouncing off the railings and clicking against each other. He nodded toward Tim. "Your turn. You're trying to sink all the solids or all the stripes. After you do that, you sink the eight ball and the game's over."

Tim went for the one ball, a solid yellow, and it dropped. He followed with two bank shots. The first went in; the second missed.

Felix stepped up to the table and lined up one of the striped balls. His shot ricocheted wildly off to the side. "Go ahead," he mumbled.

Tim sank two more before he missed. When Felix took his turn, the shot missed by a wide margin. Tim was becoming a little embarrassed. It had been Felix who suggested coming in, and Tim was beating the old man badly.

As the game went on, a wiry man drifted closer to their table. Tim saw him, but Felix didn't notice until the man was standing right next to them.

"You fellows want some competition?" the man asked.

"We're busy," Felix growled.

"You sure? I could make it worth your while."

"Get out of my way," said Felix, pushing his way past and then lining up a shot.

"See what you think of this," the man went on. "We can play eight ball. The kid here can break, then you go next. When you're finished, it'll be my turn. As soon as I

83

miss one shot, you win the game—and a hundred dollars."

"What happens if you don't miss?" Tim asked.

The man examined his fingernails. "If I run all seven of my balls—calling all of them—and then call and sink the eight ball, without missing, then he pays *me* a hundred dollars. *If* I manage to do all that without missing."

Felix eyed the newcomer. "Say, you're one of those hustler-fellows, aren't you? Well, forget it, mister. I'm nobody's fool." He turned back to the table and tried once again to line up his shot.

Without saying another word, the man pulled three crisp one-hundred-dollar bills from his wallet and placed them on the edge of the table.

Felix finished his shot, missing it badly, and looked up. "You still here?"

"Let's raise the ante," the man said. "If I don't beat you on my first turn, all three of those are yours, no questions asked. If I do beat you on my first turn, running every single one of my balls without missing, including the eight ball, then you pay me a hundred dollars. Fair enough?"

"I don't know that I could afford to lose a hundred dollars." said Felix. "Nope, sorry, mister. Go find yourself another sucker."

"How about fifty?" the man asked. "Against my three hundred?"

Felix scratched his chin. "Well, now . . ."

"Don't do it," Tim said. "He wouldn't make the bet if he wasn't sure he could win."

"Fifty dollars, huh?" Felix said. "Okay. I can afford to lose that. And I could sure use that three hundred."

"Good," said the man, "I'll rack them up." He gathered the balls into the triangle at one end of the table. Tim noticed the careless ease with which he did it, and suddenly he wished he and Felix could just walk out of the pool hall. But it was too late.

"You break, sonny," the man told him, chalking a cue stick.

Tim drove the ball hard to give Felix a wide-open break. The balls thundered and rolled to all parts of the table.

The man nodded toward Felix. "Don't bother to call your shots. You can have whatever you get. Go ahead, old man."

Tim himself thought of Felix as an old man, but he didn't like the words coming from this oily stranger. It did seem, though, that Felix suddenly looked very old indeed.

Felix circled the table awkwardly, lining up several shots and rejecting all of them. Finally he settled on a relatively easy one—the seven ball straight into the corner pocket. He closed one eye and tried it. The ball went in. Tim smiled and tried to catch Felix's eye, but the old man was too busy concentrating on his next shot. Again, it was a fairly simple shot. And again, the ball clunked into a corner pocket. They were the first two shots he had sunk all evening.

Felix wiped his forehead. He searched the table for more possibilities, but there were none—at least none that Felix had any hope of making. He looked up with a pained smile on his face. Then he shrugged and quickly lined up the first thing he saw. His stick moved forward and tapped the cue ball. The cue ball clicked against the five ball, which bounced off one rail, crossed the table, and gently caressed the three ball into the side pocket.

Suddenly Felix's whole bearing changed. He was no longer slumped over, and the apologetic smile was gone from his face. It has been replaced by a cocky grin. Felix winked at Tim. Then he proceeded to sink the remaining four balls in succession, leaving just the eight ball.

"You tricked me, old man," the stranger said quietly.

"The hustler has been hustled," Felix cackled, dropping the eight into a side pocket. He picked up the three one-hundred-dollar bills and stuffed them into his pants pocket. "Thanks for the game." He turned to Tim. "Let's get out of here, boy."

Chapter 13

As soon as they were outside, Felix whispered, "Run for it!" As they scrambled into the car and roared off down the street, Tim glanced in the rearview mirror. He saw the little man and a larger man standing in front of the pool hall. Just before Tim looked away, they walked back in.

"They won't be following us," Felix said, breathing hard. "But just to be safe, take a left here and double back to the motel on another street."

"I didn't think you were any good at pool."

"That was the whole idea."

"Did you know that would happen when we first walked in?"

Felix grinned. "Nope. But if it hadn't, you and I would

have had a pleasant game of pool. Of course, you would have won."

"I guess this'll be our last night staying at cheap motels, huh?"

The grin disappeared. "It's my money. Why should I spend it on you?"

"Hey, I'm not asking for your money. The only one who asks for stuff around here is you. You want my help, my car—well, you got them. And they're free. No charge."

The old man grunted and turned away.

They pulled into Amarillo, Texas, a little before seven o'clock Thursday evening. Felix found another run-down motel, and they rested on lumpy beds for a few minutes before going out to eat. They tried another small diner, and again the food was greasy but good.

Tim had trouble falling asleep that night, because he kept thinking about his mother. By now she'd read his note and was probably worried. He wished he'd told her more, or at least reassured her instead of making her feel bad. Finally he decided to call.

Tim got out of bed and pulled on his pants and a jacket. As he tiptoed across the room, Felix woke up.

"Where are you going?" the old man asked. Tim told him, and suddenly Felix was wide awake. "You don't want to do that."

"Why not?"

"You'll just make things worse."

Tim glanced at his watch. "It's eleven o'clock in Los

Angeles. She's home by now, and I know she's worried. I've got to call."

"Forget about Los Angeles!" Felix yelled after him. "It's a thousand miles away, and so is your mother."

Tim hurried to the pay phone and dialed 0.

"Operator 43," said a tinny voice.

"I'd like to make a collect call. The number is area code 213, 555-2118."

"What is the name, please?"

"Tim Julian."

"One moment," said the voice. Tim heard a series of high beeping noises and the ringing of a phone. He rehearsed what he'd say when his mother answered. He'd try to sound mature and unconcerned, so she'd know everything was all right. The phone kept ringing. If she pestered him about the note, he'd say it was just something he had dashed off on his way out the door.

"I'm sorry, sir, but no one answers," the voice said.

Tim looked at his watch again. "It's five after one, isn't it? So that means it's five after eleven in Los Angeles?"

"That's right."

"Keep ringing. I'm sure she's there."

The phone rang several more times, and the operator broke in again. "Please try again later."

Tim hung up and leaned against the stucco wall.

His mother wasn't home yet. She was still with Albert. Well, she could have Albert. She deserved him. They deserved each other.

"What did you tell her?" Felix asked when Tim got back.

"She's not home yet. Nobody answered."

"Looks like you'll have to get along on your own for a while," Felix chuckled. "She seems to be doing fine without you."

It was the chuckle that got to Tim. "She's not doing fine. You don't even know her. You don't know *me*."

The old man studied Tim's face, surprised by the sudden outburst.

"You haven't thought of anybody but yourself since this trip started," Tim said. "You just wanted a driver and car to get you to Chicago. When I said I was calling home, you didn't care how I was feeling. You were just worried about the trip being called off. Well, let me tell you something. If your Old Timers' Game had been the only reason for me to come, I wouldn't even be here right now." He turned away and yanked at the zipper of his jacket.

The old man sat on the edge of the bed, staring at Tim's back. After several minutes he climbed back under the covers and rolled onto his side. Long after Tim had turned off the light, Felix's eyes were still wide open.

Chapter 14

The journey from Amarillo, Texas, to Springfield, Missouri, was the longest and most grueling leg of the trip. Neither of them spoke very much the whole day. Later, thinking back on it, Tim could remember very little of what happened that Friday. It was paved from one end to the other with wide, gray turnpikes. Texas blended into Oklahoma, and Oklahoma into Missouri. Tim concentrated on driving, on chewing up the miles between him and his destination.

The one thing he remembered clearly was how he felt. He was grateful for the silence. If he'd had to talk, he wouldn't have known what to say. He couldn't go back to casual conversation about the scenery or baseball, and he had no desire to add anything to his outburst of the night before.

From the beginning of the trip, Tim had felt a steady tugging from the direction of Los Angeles. But his call home the night before had ended that. Now he could travel eastward without worrying about what he had left behind. Even though the Old Timers' Game had lost some of its appeal, it did represent a goal. It gave him somewhere to go. Besides, there was more to Chicago than baseball.

"It's home, Timmy. It's a city with a face." Bob Julian lay back on the grass of Echo Park, hands behind his head, speaking to his eleven-year-old son. Tim sat with his legs crossed, his attention riveted on his father's words. "I know it sounds corny, but Chicago's just different from most places. It's different from L.A., that's for sure."

"How?"

"It's hard to explain. Maybe part of it is that people in Chicago tend to settle in and put down roots. They get involved in the community, get to know their neighbors, watch out for each other. You don't see that around here. In L.A., as soon as people get settled in one house, they pack up their things and move on to another one."

Tim twirled a blade of grass between his fingers. "Dad, if you liked Chicago so much, why did you and Mom leave?"

"It's hard to explain."

"That's what you always say. It can't be that hard."

"Maybe not. It's just that sometimes it makes me sad. But I suppose now you're old enough to understand.

"See, Timmy, your mother never liked it there. She grew up in L.A., and her father sent her off to college in Chicago, where we met. I was managing the university bookstore in those days, and I guess she liked the idea of dating an older man—I'd reached the ripe old age of twenty-nine by that time. Before long, we were married.

"She knew how much Chicago meant to me, so there was never much of a question about where we'd live. And anyway, she had a couple of years to go yet on her college degree. I figured by that time she'd grow to like the place—how could anybody not like Chicago? But she never got used to it. The winters were tough on her; she couldn't stand that cold wind blowing off the lake. Not that she complained much—she never was that type. But I knew she didn't like it, and I felt bad about it."

"What made you decide to move?"

"Well, a few months after your mother graduated, she got sick."

"Is that when she had pneumonia?"

His father nodded. "It started out as a chest cold, but it got worse quick. That was 1964—one of the meanest winters ever. Your mother just couldn't seem to get warm, no matter how many blankets I piled on top of her, and she ended up in the hospital. She got better eventually, but she had me scared there for a while. The day she came home from the hospital I was so glad to see her that I promised we'd get out of the cold weather and move to southern California. You should have seen the look on her face, Timmy. That was when I knew for sure how much she had missed L.A. We moved that spring."

"Are you sorry you left Chicago?" Tim asked.

"Oh, not really. Chicago's a great town, but your mother's more important to me. Besides, you're happy here, right? We've got a nice house; I have a good job. Everything worked out fine."

"But you said it makes you sad sometimes."

"It does. If I told you I didn't miss Chicago, I'd be lying. But it's just a place. If you ever have to choose between a place and a person, choose the person every time. That's what I did. I wouldn't have had it any other way."

They got up a short time later and made their way back across the park. As they turned up their street, Bob Julian put his arm across his son's shoulders. "This is home, Timmy, and it's a good home. But maybe someday you'll go to Chicago. And maybe you'll feel like that's home, too."

Felix took a turn at the wheel that afternoon, barely saying a word. There was none of the usual muttering that followed every single event, big and small. At one point, a sports car cut in front of them, and the old man didn't even honk.

One thing Tim did notice was that Felix glanced over at him periodically, when he thought Tim wasn't looking. Then, afraid of being discovered, he would turn away and pretend to concentrate on his driving.

They arrived in Springfield at eight o'clock that evening. By unspoken agreement they split up and ate separately, Felix at a truck stop and Tim at a hamburger stand. Tim walked around town for an hour after dinner and then went back to the motel. He was glad to find Felix already asleep.

Saturday dawned bright and clear. Moving along Interstate 44 toward Saint Louis, Tim watched the landscape flash by. Everything was becoming greener the farther north and east they went, and Tim's mood improved with the scenery. He still didn't want to talk, but he was beginning to feel the excitement of nearing Chicago. It was hard to believe that by tonight they would be in the Windy City, looking at the sights that had surrounded Tim's father as a boy.

They drove past Saint Louis and ate lunch in Springfield, Illinois, less than two hundred miles from Chicago. Felix was at the wheel when they left Springfield. Tim noticed that the old man looked ill at ease. He kept scratching his stubbly chin and clearing his throat. Finally, a half hour after leaving the town, Felix spoke.

"By the way, what was it you said you do at that job of yours?"

"Shipping for a mail-order toy company. Why?"

"Just wondered how you like it."

"It's okay. No, I mean, it's not okay. I hate it." Tim eyed Felix. "Are you really interested?"

95

"I'm asking, aren't I? Now tell me what's wrong with it."

"My boss is terrible. His name's Mr. Martinez. When things go wrong he likes to blame other people, and I'm usually the one standing there."

Felix nodded, looking at the road. "Same thing happens to me. I had one job—" He caught himself. "How long you been working there?"

"Two years," said Tim, "but I'm thinking of leaving."

"How come?"

"Martinez accused me of stealing. That's one reason I decided to come on this trip." The old man nodded and drove on.

When they got to Joliet, about an hour outside Chicago, Felix asked Tim to drive. They switched, and Felix scanned the area for familiar sights. "That's the town my sister-in-law lived in," he said at one point. Then later: "I used to shoot some pool there." "Arnie Moses's folks had a house there." "I miss this place. Except in the winter." "Look at that—not a mountain for miles around. Chicago's flat as a board." "This expressway is new. I don't remember it."

As they went through the outlying areas of Chicago, Tim didn't notice anything much different from other suburbs he had seen. Maybe the architecture was a little different: The houses tended to be made of brick rather than stucco, and most of them looked older than houses in Los Angeles. It suddenly occurred to Tim that he might not even like Chicago, or worse, that he might simply find it dull. Maybe you'll feel like Chicago's home, too, his father had said. What if Tim didn't feel that way at all?

They neared the city itself about five o'clock, and Felix strained to see the skyline. "Look at those buildings! They're bigger than ever. See the one sticking up above the rest? That's the new Sears Building. I hear it's the tallest in the world."

The expressway took them right next to Chicago's downtown area, and now it was Tim's turn to gawk, twisting his neck to take in everything he could. There were so many tall buildings that the streets were dark with shadows. To Tim, the shadows gave the place a feeling of depth and solidity that Los Angeles lacked. The feeling was enhanced by the fact that many of the buildings were quite old. Tim's father and grandfather and perhaps even his great-grandfather had seen much the same sight.

"There's Lake Michigan," Felix said. "Even during the summer there's a cool breeze blowing off it. Can you feel it, boy?"

The highway curved left, taking them along the edge of the lake, still skirting the city. They drove past beautiful parks, and beyond they could see sailboats skimming across the water. Felix told Tim where to get off the highway, and soon they were headed away from the lake and into the city.

Tim didn't know where they were going, but he wasn't surprised when between two apartment buildings he caught a glimpse of a sign that said CHICAGO CUBS. The

97

view widened to reveal an old structure made up of brown bricks and taking up several city blocks.

Felix said, "There's the greatest ball park in the world—Wrigley Field."

Chapter 15

"That'll be seven dollars," the woman at the ticket window said.

"Don't you have anything but general admission?" Felix asked.

"Sorry. Even those are going fast. We'll be sold out by game time."

They each gave the woman three dollars and fifty cents. Tim took both tickets and slid them into his shirt pocket.

"I still don't see why we need two tickets," Tim said as they turned away from the window. "If you're going to sneak in back, all we'll need is one ticket for me."

"That's if everything goes just right," Felix replied. "But I've got a back-up plan, and I need a ticket for that."

"What's the back-up plan?"

"Well now, hold on. You don't even know the first plan yet. Come on over here, and I'll explain everything." Walking stiffly, Felix led Tim around the outside of the stadium. "See that door over by the parking lot? That's the players' entrance, and I've walked through it plenty of times. Tomorrow I'm going through it again."

"Won't they have guards?"

"Sure they will, but I'll outsmart them. I'll wait right here and watch everybody go in—new and old players both. As soon as I see a player from my day, I'll go up and say hello, then just walk in the entrance with him. If the guards try to stop me, I'll tell them I lost my pass and have the other player vouch for me. Course, the guards'll probably recognize me anyway."

"Sounds pretty easy."

"Yup. You and me will come out here by the players' entrance tomorrow morning at eleven o'clock, an hour before the Old Timers' Game. I'll have a satchel with my uniform and glove and shoes. Once I get through that door and onto the field, it's just me and my fans. They'll remember me, even if the front office doesn't."

"Why do you need a back-up plan? And why do you need me here at eleven o'clock?"

"To watch in case something goes wrong. Suppose I don't see one of my old teammates. Suppose the guards want to get technical about me not having a pass. It's possible. If that happens, I'll walk around to the front with you and go into general admission. Once I'm inside, there are ways of getting onto the field. It's not easy, but it can be done. It has to be before the Old Timers' Game, though. Once it starts, there's no way to get down there without a security guard catching you. That's why it's so important for us to be here tomorrow at eleven o'clock sharp."

They retraced their steps and returned to the car. Tim opened the trunk and put both tickets into his suitcase, just to be safe.

"There's a good hotel about three quarters of a mile from here," the old man said. "It's called the Norsted. I used to live there when I was with the Cubs. Go straight ahead, then take a left on Broadway. You'll see it."

Tim did as he was told, and on his left he spotted a faded sign on the side of an old brick building.

NORSTED HOTEL
TRANSIENT ROOMS
REASONABLE RATES

"Is this it?" he asked, looking up at the dingy three-story building.

Felix peered through the windshield. "Doesn't look too good. This place used to be a nice neighborhood hotel. Now look at it. Well, at least it'll be cheap."

They parked across the street and got out. As they did, a sign in an adjacent parking lot caught Tim's eye.

MARIGOLD BOWL
828 W. GRACE ST.
CUSTOMER PARKING ONLY

"I don't believe it," he said.

"What's that?"

"You go ahead and register for both of us. I'll be back in a minute." The old man got his two bags out of the car and went across the street to the hotel.

The Marigold Bowl—Tim had heard his father talking about this place hundreds of times. He found the bowling alley just half a block away and pushed open the door. He was greeted by a musty odor and the intermittent crash of bowling pins. As his eyes adjusted to the dim light, he made out a few shadowy figures slouched by the front desk. To the left, the lanes themselves stood empty except for two or three groups of bowlers. Tim's father often must have been greeted by the same sight when he had entered the Marigold Bowl forty years before.

Tim realized he had been standing there for several minutes. By now Felix was probably waiting for him at the hotel desk. There would be time to explore the Marigold Bowl later.

He went back to the car and got his suitcase from the trunk. Then he crossed the street to the Norsted Hotel and went inside. There was no one at the desk but a clerk reading a paperback novel.

"Did my friend come in here?" Tim asked. "He's an older man, wearing a blue shirt."

"Let's see—Felix Johnson?" the clerk looked down at the hotel register. "He signed in just a second ago. Said he was with a friend. If you're the friend, you'll need to sign, too. He couldn't remember your name."

102

"What?" Tim stepped closer to the desk and examined the register. Where his name should have been, there was just a blank space. It occurred to him that until tonight, he had always been the one to sign them into motels. It also occurred to him, now that he thought about it, that Felix had never called him by name.

Tim scribbled his name after Felix's. "Where did he go?"

"Up to the room," the clerk replied.

Tim found Felix standing at the window. The young man dropped his luggage with a thud.

Felix turned around, an expression of disgust on his face. "Look at this view. The whole neighborhood's changed."

"What's my name?"

"Huh?"

"What's my name?"

The old man shrugged and smiled sheepishly "You know how it is. Sometimes a name's right on the tip of your tongue—a name you know as well as your own. It's a crazy thing. It's like—"

Felix didn't finish the sentence, because there was no one else left in the room to hear it.

Tim sped through the city streets, hunched over the steering wheel, not even sure where he was going. He was looking at the roadway, but he was still seeing the old man by the window, smiling foolishly, trying to think of an excuse for having forgotten his name.

I'm the one, Tim thought, who remembered the base-

103

ball with his name on it. I'm the one who tracked him down by making long-distance phone calls and writing letters. I'm the one who left home to drive him all the way to Chicago. And he doesn't even know my name.

Tim turned a corner and found himself back at Wrigley Field. It was six thirty—a good two hours before sunset—so he parked the car and wandered around the perimeter of the park.

The block he was on was where Bob Julian had grown up. Tim remembered hearing his father describe a next-door apartment building with a flat, fenced-in roof, where once a week he and his friends had been allowed to sit and look over the right-field wall to see the action. Tim recalled his father's description of one afternoon when the great Gabby Hartnett had homered over that wall, right into the waiting glove of Bob Julian's best friend. The ball had become a neighborhood treasure, along with Bob Julian's souvenir baseball signed by Felix the Great.

Tim looked up at the block-long row of apartment buildings. He wondered which had been his father's home as a boy and which had been the next-door building with the fenced-in roof. He walked slowly down the sidewalk and toward the end of the block came upon a red brick apartment building. On the porch, an old couple sat in a swing, surveying the neighborhood.

"Beautiful day, eh?" the man called out to Tim.

"Yes, sir."

"I love summer, don't you?" the man asked. Tim nodded, smiling. "Come up closer. We're not going to bite you."

Tim moved up the walk to the porch. He saw now that the old man was wearing tweed pants, a white shirt, and bright-red suspenders. The woman sitting next to him had on a flower print dress.

"This weather sure beats winter, doesn't it?" said the man.

"I guess so," Tim replied. "But I wouldn't know. I don't live here."

"What brings you to town?"

"Henry," the old woman said, "maybe he doesn't feel like telling you his life story." She turned to Tim. "He's always trying to rope people into talking with him. You don't have to if you don't want to."

"It's okay," Tim said. "I'm here for the Old Timers' Game tomorrow. I came to this neighborhood because it's where my father grew up. Maybe you knew him— Bob Julian?"

The woman shook her head. "We've only lived here two years."

"Do you know anyone who's been here for a long time—forty years or so?" Tim asked.

"Can't think of a one," the man replied. "I wish we could help you, but you know how it is. People move on, especially these days. It used to be different, I'll tell you that. People would grow up in a neighborhood and then stay there. That's the way it should be."

The woman chuckled. "Tell the young man how many times we've moved in the past ten years, Henry."

The old man scratched behind his ear. "Oh, maybe once or twice."

"We've moved four times," she pronounced triumphantly. "And I'm glad we did. I like a change of scenery once in a while, and so do you, Henry. Don't waste the young man's time with your front-porch philosophy. The good old days are gone, and that's that."

"Maybe I did get a little carried away," he admitted.

"Anyway, young man," she went on, "I'm sure you've got better things to do than listen to a couple of old coots argue with each other."

"That's okay, it's interesting. I mean, I've enjoyed talking to you."

"Our pleasure, son," the old man replied. "Sorry we couldn't help you find out about your father. It's just that forty years is a long time."

Chapter 16

After leaving the old couple, Tim wandered farther down the block. He had the feeling that if he just looked closely enough, he would catch a glimpse of his father's world: maybe a child's face in a window; a Chicago Cub cap perched on someone's head; a game of catch on the sidewalk. He kept going until he had circled Wrigley Field and arrived back where he began. There he remembered the Marigold Bowl.

Tim drove back and parked near the bowling alley, half a block from the Norsted Hotel. It would have been easier to use the lot across from the hotel, but Tim was afraid Felix might spot him.

The Marigold Bowl was as dimly lighted as ever, and it took a few moments for Tim's eyes to adjust to the darkness. When they did, he saw a few bowlers, some listless spectators, and a small group of people lounging around the front desk.

"Can I help you, buddy?" the man behind the desk called.

"I guess not." Tim picked up his pace and, not knowing what else to do, headed for the candy machine. The chocolate bars shown in the little window had turned white with age. He moved off in the other direction.

There were tattered theater seats in rows facing the lanes, and Tim slipped into one of them. He looked down on two bowlers his own age. Maybe they were using the same lane his father had used; maybe one of the scuffed bowling balls had been his dad's favorite.

"Pardon me." A man was moving across the row toward Tim, sweeping as he went.

"Sure," Tim mumbled, and pulled up his knees. "Nice bowling alley."

"Good joke," said the sweeper. "I like that." The smell of liquor was strong on his breath.

"I wasn't kidding. Probably a lot of people have had a good time here."

The man settled into a chair, propping the broom against his leg. "Maybe a few have. I suppose it's possible."

Tim saw that the man was much younger than he had seemed at first, probably not over forty. "How long have you worked here?" he asked.

"Year and a half. And that was just this week. I don't think I'll ever get used to sweeping floors. I'm not the

108

janitor type. I used to live up on Lake Shore Drive. Had a high-rise apartment, one of those penthouses that look out over the lake." He drew himself up straight, then settled back down like a deflated balloon. "You don't believe me."

"Sure I do."

"Good, just checking. See, I was an engineer. Used to invent things. I made a lot of money, too. Around here they laugh when I say that, but I swear on my broom it's true.

"You're probably wondering what happened, right?" the man said. "You're a nice kid, and you wouldn't come out and ask, but I can tell. Well, I hit on some hard times, and things went sour. I lost my job, I had to move out of that apartment, and pretty soon my savings were almost gone. I don't really blame anybody. It just happened. I won't bore you with the details, but let's just say that within three years I was duke of the dust bin.

"What about you?" asked the man. "You don't fit in. What are you doing here?"

"Just looking around the neighborhood," Tim said.

"Don't waste your time. The bowling alley, the flophouses, the seedy bars, the lousy stadium—I wouldn't give you a nickel for all of them. People around here don't know what class is. Class is Lake Shore Drive, and I used to live there." Bowling pins cracked and echoed in the background. "Sorry, kid, I didn't mean to get carried away. I haven't had an audience for a long time."

"That's okay."

"Tell you what," said the floor sweeper. "Let me buy

you a Coke. You deserve it for putting up with me."

They went over to the machine, where the man put in a coin and handed Tim a soft drink.

"Aren't you having one?" Tim asked.

"Nah, I never drink on the job."

"What the hell are you doing?" asked a loud voice behind them. They turned and saw the man from the front desk.

"Just showing this kid where the soft-drink machine is."

"I pay you to sweep floors, not give guided tours." The man wheeled around and walked off.

"He's really a nice guy once you get to know him," said Tim's friend. "Unfortunately, nobody knows him."

"Sorry I got you in trouble."

"No problem. I'd better get back to work, though. I can hear the dustballs calling."

An hour later Tim was still in the alley. Lost in thought, he was startled by a tapping on his shoulder. It was the floor sweeper.

"I just got off work and wanted to tell you something before I leave. The guy behind the desk doesn't like people hanging around unless they're his friends, so you might want to move on. But if you need to come back later, wait until after midnight. A friend of mine works the desk from then until eight, and the guy after that isn't too bad, either. Neither of them will bother you. Okay?"

"I really appreciate it, mister."

The floor sweeper offered his hand uncertainly, as

though no longer sure what the gesture meant. Tim shook it firmly and said, "I hope things work out for you."

"Are you kidding? I lead a charmed life." The floor sweeper walked toward the exit, weaving ever so slightly. As he reached the door, he straightened his shoulders, then went on through.

Tim waited a few minutes and then left. It was almost nine o'clock, and yet outside the air was still hot and muggy. He saw a hamburger stand and, realizing he was hungry, ate dinner sitting on the curb. Afterward, he walked.

The sky had grown dark, and the lights of the neighborhood were on. With them came sounds—mellow jazz on the radio, the laughter of a baby, a distant police siren, a vacuum cleaner. Tim tried to reconcile the appearance of the neighborhood with the bleak scene the floor sweeper had described, and to reconcile both with the rosy pictures his father had conjured up. The floor sweeper saw the place as a grimy purgatory, populated by bums and hustlers, to which he had been sentenced by bad luck. Bob Julian saw a paradise where people lived in harmony, knitted together by a common love for the city and the Cubs. But what Tim saw was just a place to live. People laughed, people argued, people hurt each other, people helped each other—they did all the things people do in Los Angeles or Toledo or Des Moines.

Somehow it made Tim sad. He had hoped to find something different, a place where he would feel at home. He had hoped to find something of his father.

But his father wasn't here. He wasn't in Los Angeles, and he wasn't in Chicago. He was gone.

Tim slowed down and stopped in the darkness between streetlights. He remained there for several minutes. Then he lifted his head and moved on into the night.

Chapter 17

When Felix woke up, he knew something was wrong.

In the early morning light he strained to look at the other bed in the dingy hotel room. The bed hadn't been slept in. Worse, the boy's suitcase still stood by the door where he had dropped it the afternoon before. Felix had lifted the tag on the suitcase. *Tim Julian* it said. Was that so hard to remember?

After Tim had left the room yesterday, Felix had started to follow him and then decided against it. The last time Tim was angry with him, the boy had left for a few hours and then come back late that night, after Felix had fallen asleep. Felix had decided that this time would probably be no different. As soon as Tim calmed down, he would return to the hotel and get a good night's sleep for the big day ahead.

But now it was obvious Felix had been wrong. Of all the nights not to come back, why had Tim chosen this one? Felix needed him. Where was the boy?

Muttering to himself, Felix walked over to his suitcase and pulled out his shaving kit. He carried it across the room to the broken-down sink and began to shave. Watching himself in the discolored mirror, he wondered where Tim could be. There were plenty of things that could happen to a teenager in downtown Chicago in the middle of the night, and few of them were good.

His thoughts were interrupted by the shrill wailing of a police siren. Still holding his razor, Felix stumbled over to the window. He peered through the caked dirt but couldn't see the police car. Where was it going? Had there been an accident, a kidnapping, a killing? *Where was the boy?*

Felix dressed quickly and packed his suitcase, then opened his shoulder bag. His cap, glove, baseball shoes, and Cub uniform were inside. He pulled the shirt out for a moment and looked at it. His old number, 17, was stitched neatly on the back, and above it Elizabeth Crawford had sewn, in matching blue letters, *Felix the Great.*

Felix folded up the shirt and put on the cap, then closed the shoulder bag. He took both suitcases down to the front desk. "We'll be back for these later," he told the clerk as he checked out. "And do you have some paper and a pencil? I want to leave the boy a note."

The clerk produced a note pad, and Felix scrawled a message on the top sheet, instructing Tim to meet him at Wrigley Field next to the players' entrance at 11:00 A.M. Then he folded the sheet, wrote *Tim Julian* on it, and handed it to the clerk.

As Felix left the hotel, he glanced at his watch and saw that it was eight fifteen. There were still almost three hours before the time when he and Tim had agreed to meet. Even so, it wouldn't hurt to go on over to Wrigley Field. Felix adjusted the strap of the shoulder bag and was suddenly thankful that the hotel was less than a mile from the stadium.

He made his way down Broadway to Waveland and turned right. It was odd walking through his old neighborhood. He passed a barber shop, two bars, a used-car lot, an old school building, a Chinese restaurant. Although he recognized individual landmarks, the overall effect was one of strangeness, like a jigsaw puzzle whose pieces had been scrambled.

Even though it was early, there were people on the streets. In contrast to Felix's purposeful gait, most of them walked aimlessly along, chatting happily, perhaps thinking of the Fourth of July holiday that lay before them. Felix scanned the pedestrians, hoping for a glimpse of Tim's T-shirt and jeans. He watched the cars, looking for a Dodge Dart.

Once, he thought he saw Tim disappear into an old apartment building. He hurried to the door and peered in. A curly-haired stranger looked back. Felix mumbled something and left.

The shoulder bag was small, but already he could feel

the effects of its weight. His shoulder and back ached, and he was developing a blister on one heel. He limped along, his eyes darting from person to person, car to car, building to building.

At last, Felix saw the stadium up ahead. He checked his watch: eight forty-five. He went to the players' entrance, but Tim wasn't there. Of course, it was early yet. The boy was probably on his way.

Felix looked around for a more comfortable place to wait and saw a doughnut shop. He bought a newspaper from the rack in front and went inside, where he picked out a table with a view of the players' entrance. Then he ordered a cup of coffee and settled down to wait.

Almost two hours later, Felix still had seen no sign of Tim. Eleven o'clock was approaching, so he got up and made his way toward the players' entrance.

As he walked, he noticed people starting to arrive. There were young couples holding hands and middle-aged men in groups of two or three studying the box scores. There were families carrying picnic baskets and thermoses. There were women wearing visors and hats, with cushions tucked under their arms. These were his fans. In just a little more than an hour, they would be cheering as he walked onto the field.

An old man with slumped shoulders moved past Felix toward the players' entrance. There was something familiar about the way he walked. Felix looked more closely and saw that it was Larry McMurphy, an old teammate. He took a step toward him and then caught himself. Perhaps Tim was just running late. Felix decided to wait a few more minutes before using his plan. There would be other friends coming along, and he would go in with them.

A few minutes passed, and a few more, and it was eleven twenty. Felix paced back and forth. The boy was probably out sightseeing or watching a parade or cruising along Michigan Avenue. Maybe he'd even decided to drive home. But why had he left his suitcase?

What's my name? Tim had said. More than the words, he remembered the expression on his face: anger, and a kind of pleading. What did the boy want from him?

It was almost eleven thirty. A lone, bald-headed man walked through the crowd toward the players' entrance. He glanced at Felix. "Johnson?" he ventured. Felix squinted back, nodding. "It's me, Arnie Moses."

"What happened to your hair?" asked Felix.

"It fell out, that's what happened to it!"

"Well, I didn't mean . . ."

Arnie grinned and slapped Felix on the shoulder. "Don't apologize, man. I would have been disappointed if you hadn't insulted me. How have you been?"

"Okay. I'm living in Los Angeles."

"Here for the game today?"

"Yeah."

"Come on, I'll walk you in."

"I can't go in yet, Arnie. I'm waiting for somebody else."

"Well, don't wait too long or you'll miss the game." Felix nodded, and his friend disappeared into the players' entrance.

He stood there for several minutes, watching the fans

117

bustle by. He remembered how they had roared their approval of Felix the Great so many years ago. Now, standing unrecognized outside the park, he tried to hear the sound in his head and couldn't.

What if Tim wasn't out sightseeing? What if he was in trouble? With great effort, Felix turned away from the players' entrance and moved off in the other direction. His shoulder ached, and he was still limping badly.

"Taxi!" he yelled, raising his free hand in the air. A cab pulled up, and Felix got in. "Take me to the nearest police station. No, take me to the Norsted Hotel first. Hurry!"

The cab lurched away from the curb and shot down the street. As it did, Felix peered out the back window and saw Wrigley Field recede into the distance.

Chapter 18

"Sonny." A voice filtered through the haze of Tim's sleep, and a hand shook his shoulder gently. "Sonny? You okay?"

Tim opened his eyes and saw a wrinkled black face looking down at him. He suddenly thought of Michael and wondered how his friend was doing. Good old Michael. It seemed like forever since he had seen him. Cal, too. Tim rubbed his eyes. "You're not Michael," he said.

The man chuckled. "That's a fact. I'm not Michael. I was worried about you, sonny. You've just been laying there in that chair ever since I came on duty, so I thought I'd check up on you. Well, now that I've checked, you can go back to sleep."

Tim stretched and sat up straight, then remembered

where he was and how he had gotten there. The night before, he had covered the entire area around the stadium. He wasn't sure why he had kept walking for so long; all he knew was at the time it had seemed important to keep moving. When he finally ran out of energy, he had headed for the Marigold Bowl and collapsed into one of their seats. Before falling asleep, he had looked at the lighted blue-and-white clock high on one wall. It had been nearly three thirty in the morning.

Now Tim looked at the clock again. It showed ten fifteen, and he was supposed to meet Felix at the stadium at eleven. Suddenly he was wide awake. "I've got to get going."

"I'm not kicking you out, sonny. I just wanted to make sure you were okay."

"Thanks, mister." He hurried outside, stopping only to splash water on his face at the drinking fountain. The streets were already crowded with traffic, so he decided to walk to Wrigley Field instead of driving. There was still enough time for him to make it on foot.

He set a brisk pace and began to notice his surroundings. It was the same neighborhood he had explored the night before, except now it was swarming with people. Yesterday, Tim had been trying to mold it to fit his father's description, but now he was content to see whatever presented itself this new day.

As his eyes ranged over the scenery, his thoughts touched on Felix Johnson. In the space of a few hours yesterday, Tim had gone from admiring the old man to hating him to feeling sorry for him. Somehow in the morning sunshine, the original goal of the trip—getting Felix into the Old Timers' Game—once again seemed important.

That was when Tim remembered the tickets.

He had put them into his suitcase the day before for safekeeping, and the suitcase was back at the hotel. For a minute he considered going to the stadium in hopes of getting new tickets, but he decided the holiday game was certainly sold out by now. Luckily, there was enough time to walk to the hotel, get the tickets, and still make it back to Wrigley Field by eleven o'clock. Since the car was parked nearby, he could even drive to the stadium if he needed to.

Fifteen minutes later he was back at the hotel, where a different clerk sat behind the desk.

"Did Felix Johnson check out yet?" Tim asked.

The clerk looked at the register. "Yes, he did, about eight o'clock this morning."

"Do you happen to know what he did with his suitcases?"

"Matter of fact, he left them here. Why?"

"One of them is mine," Tim said. "I need to get something out of it."

"What's your name?"

"Tim Julian."

"Julian." The man shuffled through some papers. "I thought I recognized that name. Here's a note for you."

121

Tim read Felix's note quickly, stuffed it into his pocket, and reached for his suitcase.

"Oh, and there was a phone call for you just a minute ago." He pulled out another note. "The person wants you to call back."

"Was it Felix Johnson?"

"No, it must have been a relative. Somebody named Bonnie Julian."

"What?"

"She left a number. You want it?"

Tim shook his head. "I already know it. It's my home number in California."

The clerk handed Tim the note. "No, you're wrong there. It's local."

Bonnie Julian stood in the Chicago Cubs' public-relations office, adjoining Wrigley Field. Fred Ballantine, the Cubs' publicity director, was pacing back and forth across the office. His secretary seemed to be the only calm person in the room.

"More coffee, Mrs. Julian?" she asked.

"No, thanks," Bonnie replied. "I'm jumpy enough as it is." She studied the Cub photos that hung on the walls and thought back to the events of the past five days.

She had been concerned about Tim ever since Tuesday when she and Albert set off on their trip. She felt better by the time they reached their hotel in Santa Barbara, but she had called Tim that evening just to make sure everything was all right. There was no answer. She and Albert went out to dinner, and she called once more Wednesday morning. Again there was no answer. She tried again Wednesday night and early Thursday morning, with the same results. By that time, concern had grown into fear.

Deciding to cut their trip short, they hurried back to Los Angeles and arrived late Thursday morning. That was when they found Tim's note.

All afternoon she and Albert searched the house for clues as to where he could have gone. Finally Bonnie came across a copy of Tim's "Where Are They Now?" paper and read about how Tim had visited Felix Johnson at the Alvarado Retirement Home. On a hunch, she looked up the phone number and called. When she asked for Mr. Johnson, she was told he had left town Wednesday morning with a friend.

She and Albert hurried over to the home and ended up speaking to Elizabeth Caldwell, who remembered Tim from his visit there. Caldwell said Felix Johnson had told her they were going to the Old Timers' Game in Chicago.

By that time, it was almost eleven o'clock Thursday night, so the two of them went to a coffee shop and discussed what to do. Bonnie's first impulse was to find Tim and bring him home. But another part of her said to wait a few days. She was still undecided when she went to bed that night.

Early Friday morning she called the Cub office and spoke to Fred Ballantine in public relations. He told her the Old Timers' Game would be held on July 4, Sunday, at noon. He also mentioned that, so far as he knew, Felix

Johnson wasn't scheduled to be in it. But he said he would alert the Wrigley Field staff to keep an eye out for Tim and Felix during the next few days and would call Bonnie immediately if he learned anything. Ballantine even volunteered to have an announcement made over the public address system during the game if the two of them hadn't appeared by then.

She thanked him and said good-bye. Then began the hard part: waiting. Every time the phone rang, she jumped to answer it. Every time the doorbell chimed, she raced to see who was there. When the mail arrived, she greeted the postman at the door. After two days of that, she decided she couldn't wait any longer.

By Saturday night she was on a plane to Chicago, and by Sunday she was in the public-relations office at Wrigley Field. She had been waiting almost three hours with Ballantine for some word about whether Tim or Felix had been seen.

There was a knock at the door.

Ballantine opened it, and there in the hallway stood Jake, the clubhouse custodian, with an older man wearing a baseball uniform.

"My name's Lester Marco," the player said. "Jake here tells me Felix Johnson's in town and everybody's looking for him."

"Have you seen him?" Ballantine asked.

"No, nothing like that," the man said. "There was one thing, though. He and Arnie Moses used to stay at the Norsted Hotel. Felix really loved the place. You might call there, just on the off chance he might have gone back."

Ballantine looked at Bonnie, and she nodded. It was better than sitting and doing nothing.

Chapter 19

Tim went to the pay phone in the hotel hallway and dialed the number. "Good morning. Chicago Cubs. Mr. Ballantine's office."

"Chicago Cubs?" Tim asked. "I must have the wrong number. Is there a Bonnie Julian there?"

"There certainly is. Just a minute."

A moment later, his mother came on the line. "Tim, is that you?"

"What are you doing here?"

"What am *I* doing here? I traveled two thousand miles to ask you the same question."

"But how did you know where to find me? How come you're at the Cub office?"

"I'd rather tell you in person," his mother replied. "Are you calling from that hotel? The Norsted?"

"Uh-huh."

"Just wait right there. I'll be right over."

"Mom—"

She hung up before he could say any more. He had wanted to tell her he'd drive to Wrigley Field and see her there, so he could keep his eleven o'clock meeting with Felix, but now he'd just have to skip the meeting. Luckily, Tim didn't play an important part in Felix's plan. The old man could get in by himself, and Tim would be at the stadium by twelve o'clock to see the Old Timers' Game.

Tim wandered back to the deserted lobby and flopped down onto a well-worn couch. Fifteen minutes later the door burst open, and Bonnie Julian hurried inside. She rushed across the room and hugged him.

"I was so worried about you," she said. Then the tone of her voice changed. "What were you doing, running off like that? I was scared to death."

"You didn't seem too scared Thursday night. I tried calling at eleven o'clock, but you weren't even home yet. You told me you'd be back Thursday afternoon."

"I was back Thursday morning, looking for you, and I didn't get home until after midnight. That's why no one answered." She sketched the events of the past few days, then demanded, "Why did you do it?"

"I don't have to ask you every time I leave the house," he said.

"You left the state!"

"You didn't ask *my* permission to go to Santa Barbara with Albert."

"No, but at least I told you I was going. You could

127

have done the same—unless the whole point was to make me feel bad."

"That's ridiculous."

Bonnie pulled the note from her purse. " 'There's no reason for me to stay around here. You'll be with Albert.' "

"Okay, maybe that was the point. Maybe I don't like what you've been doing."

"Which is?"

"Being gone all the time. Seeing too much of that guy Albert."

"It all comes back to him, doesn't it?"

"Yeah, I guess."

"Give him a chance, Tim."

"Why?"

"Because you're wrong. He's very different from your father, but he's a wonderful man."

"He's not going to take Dad's place."

"Come on, that's not what you're worried about. You're afraid he'll take your place."

"What's that supposed to mean?"

"Tim, after your father died, I depended on you. Not just for money from your job, but for emotional support, too."

"I didn't mind."

"I know, and that meant a lot to me. But now you can put down some of the load, or at least learn to share it. I've got my own life, and you've got yours. I'm sure there are girls you want to date, and things you want to do besides work. Things have changed, Tim. Maybe it's time we both grew up."

128

Tim rose from the couch and walked a few feet away, where he stood with his arms crossed.

"What are you thinking?" his mother asked.

"I'm thinking of home. I'm tired of sleeping in lumpy beds."

She got up and kissed her son on the cheek. He put one arm clumsily around her shoulders.

Just then, Felix Johnson entered the room.

Chapter 20

"What in blazes are you doing here?" Felix yelled, dropping his shoulder bag on the floor. "You were supposed to be at Wrigley Field at eleven!"

"I was going to come, but my mother called. She flew in from Los Angeles."

"I don't care where she flew in from! We had an agreement."

"I figured you could get in without me, and then I'd see you at the game. Did something go wrong?"

"Yeah—you! You didn't show up. So like an idiot I had to go looking for you. I just stopped by here on my way to the police station."

"You were worried?"

130

"No, I was not worried!" Felix said. "Where were you last night?"

"Over at the bowling alley. I was fine."

"You could have called and told me that. If you had, I'd be standing out on the field right now."

Tim looked at his watch. "There's still five minutes left before the game."

"It's too late. All my friends are inside the clubhouse already, and once the game starts, you can't get to the field from the stands. There's no way to do it now." His voice trailed off, and his shoulders sagged.

"I'm sorry, Mr. Johnson."

"Well, let's at least go watch the game," said Tim's mother. She pulled three tickets from her purse. "Mr. Ballantine gave me these. They're right behind the Cubs' dugout."

"Want to go, Mr. Johnson?" asked Tim.

Felix scratched his chin. "I got nothing better to do," he mumbled.

They drove to Wrigley Field and squeezed into a lot a block from the stadium. Tim and his mother wanted to hurry but didn't have the heart to urge the old man on, so the group moved slowly.

At the gate, a woman took their tickets and waved them on. The area underneath the grandstand was over-run with people. Fans scurried back and forth, carrying peanuts and hot dogs and beer. Concessionaires hawked programs and souvenirs.

The three travelers snaked their way through the crowd, Tim first, his mother following, and Felix trailing

131

listlessly behind. As they neared the top of the aisle, Tim caught his first glimpse of what had enchanted his father forty years before: the inside of Wrigley Field.

Tim could see why Felix didn't like Dodger Stadium. The difference between it and Wrigley Field was the difference between an office and a home.

The grass seemed much greener here. The dirt of the infield was browner. The baselines and batters' boxes, as yet unused, were perfectly neat and white. And the fences were ivy-covered walls. These were the same walls Felix had peppered with line drives so many years ago. And they were the same walls over which his father had viewed Saturday-afternoon games as a boy. Beyond right field Tim could see people sitting on apartment roofs, one of which was doubtless the very same roof where his father had sat.

On the field stood a line of players, stretched between home plate and first base just outside the foul line. Some of their uniforms were too tight; others were baggy and had to be cinched up at the belt. A few of the players were stooped a bit, and gray hair poked out from under several hats. These were the old timers.

As Tim led the way through the crowd and down the aisle, he became aware of the public address announcer's voice. ". . . played right field for the Cubs from 1938 through 1945—Millard Carney!" There was applause, and one of the players stepped forward and tipped his cap.

"And next . . ." The announcer continued down the list of old timers.

Felix Johnson would not be on the list. That was the

fault of the Cub management. He wouldn't be on the field, either. And that, Tim decided, was the fault of Tim Julian. He had traveled over two thousand miles to bring Felix to Wrigley Field for this moment and had let him down. Beyond all the complications and excuses, that was the simple truth.

When they reached their seats, Tim's mother leaned over and squeezed his arm. "I'm glad we're here," she said.

The introductions ended, and the game started. The big Fourth of July crowd responded to every play, every move, every flash of old form. The announcer kept up a lively running commentary, recalling past heroics and paying tribute to each old timer.

Tim looked at Felix. The old man's blank expression had turned sullen. His eyes were narrowed, and his mouth was set in a thin, straight line.

"Ladies and gentlemen," said the announcer, "we have another old timer with us today, someone who wasn't able to play in the game but who should be introduced anyway. He played shortstop for the Cubs from 1927 to 1941 and was one of our all-time greats, both at bat and in the field. He drove all the way from Los Angeles just to be with us today, and let's show him how much we appreciate it. Seated just a few rows behind the Cubs' dugout, please welcome Felix Johnson—better known as Felix the Great!"

With the mention of his name, Felix started.

"That's you, Mr. Johnson," said Tim. "Stand up, that's you!" He turned to his mother. "How did they know?"

"Mr. Ballantine arranged it." She said to Felix, "Come on, Mr. Johnson."

Slowly Felix struggled to his feet. As he did, a low rumble started among the nearby fans, and it spread through the section, across the aisles, and around the stadium. Heads turned, and a few people stood up to peer in their direction.

A shy grin formed on Felix's lips. He reached up, fumbled with the bill of his cap, and lifted it off his head. The rumble was now mixed with applause, scattered at first and then more pronounced. There were whistles and cheers. "There he is," someone yelled. "Felix the Great!"

More people got to their feet, straining to see. The cheers grew louder, and Felix's grin widened. He held the cap high over his head and slowly wheeled from left to right, taking in the sweep of the holiday crowd. As he did, the long, bitter years seemed to drop away, and Felix felt as if he had never left Wrigley Field and the Cubs. In his mind, the cheers became a roar, a wall of sound surrounding and supporting him. He waved his cap back and forth, harder and harder, as though ringing the bell of some great cathedral.

The cheering died down, and people took their seats once again. Felix gave his cap one last wave, then settled shakily back into his chair, his eyes glistening. As he did, a little boy in a Cub cap approached him. The boy had a baseball in one hand and a pen in the other.

"Mr. Johnson," he said, "could you sign this for me?"

Felix glanced at Tim, uncertain of what to do, then he turned back to the boy.

134

"What's your name?" Felix asked.

"Tony."

Felix took the ball and pen. "We'll call you Tony the Great. Just like me, Felix the Great."

The old man leaned over and with infinite care began to autograph the baseball.

About the Author

"Somehow, in spite of the strikes and salary disputes, there's still something magical about baseball," writes author Ronald Kidd. "When I go to the ball park and look down on the clipped grass and the white lines and the players moving in the sunshine, I feel like a boy again. For a moment it seems as if things used to be perfect and still can be, if only I give myself over to the game. This book is the story of a young man and an old man who together try to do just that."

Mr. Kidd is the author of *Dunker, That's What Friends Are For*, and several other books. He also writes and produces films and filmstrips for schools. He and his wife live in Altadena, California.